Anne-Marie Drosso

A nne-Marie Drosso was born in Cairo, Egypt, in 1951. She left in her early twenties for Vancouver, Canada, studying for her Ph.D in Economics, and later completed a Law degree. In 1999, Drosso began writing fiction after returning to Egypt. Her first release was the short story collection, *Cairo Stories* (Telegram Books, 2007), followed by her first novel, *In Their Father's Country* (Telegram Books, 2009). Drosso now resides in Vancouver.

ANNE-MARIE DROSSO

Hookah Nights

DARF PUBLISHERS,
LONDON

Published by Darf Publishers 2018

Darf Publishers Ltd.
277 West End Lane
West Hampstead
London
NW6 1QS

Hookah Nights
By Anne-Marie Drosso

Cover designed by Luke Pajak

Printed and bound in Great Britain by Clays Ltd, St Ives plc

ISBN-13: 978-1-85077-314-6
eBook ISBN: 978-1-85077-315-3

This is a work of fiction. Names, characters, businesses, places,
events and incidents are either the products of the author's
imagination or used in a fictional manner.

www.darfpublishers.co.uk

Hookah Nights

Good Man

That particular morning, carpeted by grit, Cairo's streets were deserted; shutters and windows were tightly closed. It was the end of March. The first *khamaseen* of the season was blowing over the city, driving its residents indoors. Later in the day, after the hot, dry, wind-bearer of dust and sand had died down, there would be the usual disagreement amongst Cairenes as to whether it was the worst *khamaseen* ever, or nothing compared to previous ones – a mere child's *khamaseen*.

The day following a *khamaseen* is one of drudgery in homes. Floors, surfaces, and drawers need to be wiped, rugs and carpets shaken, shoes polished, clothes and even undergarments washed. It is a wretched wind, the only good thing that may be said about it is that it either announces or coincides with the beginning of spring and Sham el-Nessim, for poor and rich Egyptians alike a day of family picnics – weather permitting. Sham el-Nessim would be especially feted this year. Having come through the Suez Crisis unbowed six months earlier, Egypt was still priding itself on having humbled Great Britain, France and Israel.

As the wind gathered strength outside, the Canadian ambassador, seated at his desk, was staring at a couch across his office. He hadn't bothered switching the lights on even though the shutters were closed. In his hand was a letter from a colleague in Ottawa he had yet to respond to, and which he was in turn crumpling and smoothing. The couch on which his eyes were fixed was long enough for him to stretch out fully without having to bend his knees, not something a man his height could do on a standard couch, and it was wide and firm enough for him to lie on his back, instead of curled up on his side.

He had not slept in days, certainly not the past three nights. If he did what he promised himself not to do, it would be the third – no – fourth consecutive morning that he would lie on the couch with his eyes shut tight, his head throbbing and mind racing.

Before leaving the office the previous night, he had scribbled in his diary, 'The couch must go. The embassy's new hire should be able to move it in the morning.' It occurred to him that the new employee, a beaming young man he had met briefly, must have arrived in the office and might be free to remove it.

He continued to stare at the couch. The letter from Ottawa slipped from his hand. He did not pick it up. When he finally bestirred himself, it was to tear into ever-smaller pieces a blank sheet of paper lying on his desk. What should he say to his colleague in Ottawa who had taken the trouble to write him this sympathetic letter of support, and even gone over old history, insisting that, in 1951, the Canadian government should have stuck to its guns, ignored the Americans' request that he be moved and kept him as Canada's representative at the UN? Should he agree with his solicitous colleague or defend the government's action? Pearson had stood by him, and still did, but would likely pay a price for it. If only he and Pearson had spoken the simple truth when questions were first raised and aspersions cast; if only they had admitted his brief flirtation with communism. The ridiculousness of it all!

The bits of paper were so small now that there was nothing more to shred. He needed to put his head down, so he cleared a space on his desktop and lay his forearms there to cushion his brow. There was no chance that he would feel well enough for his usual game of tennis later in the day, he thought, as he breathed in some dust. Fortunately, the weather meant tennis was out of the question.

The *khamaseen* – a first for him – could be his excuse for lying down. *Khamaseens* are known to induce lethargy. 'The ambassador is resting,' he imagined his staff telling each other since somebody was bound to come into his office at some point and see him stretched out on the couch. Once out of the office, that person would probably remark with a sympathetic pity the thought of which made him cringe, 'He's been so busy, no wonder he's exhausted.'

True, he had had a lot on his plate. Before arriving, he had been warned that Egypt would not be an easy posting. He had come prepared to work hard, all the more so that he did not know Arabic. He still believed that, without knowledge of its language, one's understanding of a country is bound to remain limited. He would concede, however, that he had not done a bad job in Egypt.

Many said he was doing a superb job, in fact. The information was filtering through that Nasser's acceptance of Canadian peacekeepers on Egyptian soil was largely thanks to him striking the right note during their last meeting. He had drawn an analogy between Canada and Egypt, depicting both countries as anxious to assert independence and chart their own courses. His own palpable attachment to Japan may also have played a role in softening Nasser, since Egypt's foreign minister had spent several years in Kobe. Such things can matter, even if they should not.

Yet success is not the same as fulfilment. A diplomat's work can engender a sense of futility and the loss of an independent perspective. In the past few weeks, he had been all too conscious of those perils and had tried his best not to lose sight of what was right as opposed to expedient. 'The situation in the Middle East made it hard not to become pessimistic,' he had written in a letter still to be mailed to his brother. He had gone on to say that with as intransigent a neighbour as Israel, Arab nations were bound to be worried, and the temptation for their leaders would be to exploit Israel's existence to consolidate their power. He feared the dangerous dynamics that might ensue.

Yes, these had been hectic and stressful weeks. Shortly after his arrival in Cairo, someone had told him to expect his first six months in the city to be exciting, then a feeling of estrangement would grip him and he would begin to wonder what he was doing in Egypt at all. Then he would gradually mellow, without ever being quite as excited and inspired as he'd been at the outset. Was he simply going through the phase of finding it hard to adjust to Egypt?

He wished that were the case, but no – Egypt was not the reason he was feeling drained, helpless, demoralised, already defeated. It would be unfair to blame Egypt for his overwhelming fatigue and desire to crawl into bed, pull a thick blanket over his head and shut everything out. Strange how his desire to hide was coupled with an urge to have someone listen to him express his disgust, anger, and dread about what was to come. Perhaps what he feared most was that in the renewed grilling to which he would be subjected, he risked disavowing old friends such as Cornford and Maclauren, men of valour who had died for a cause, misguided or not, whereas he had chosen to live. Time had not quite erased his feeling that he ought to atone for having stayed out of a war in which his friends had died. It did not matter that he no longer believed in their cause, which had been his too, briefly.

Before restarting their campaign and branding him a traitor, or at the very least a potential traitor, his accusers seemed to have waited for him to do some solid work he could be proud of. For the past twenty-four hours, he had been haunted by the image of a man just let out of jail walking towards a bar, already savouring in his mind his first sip of scotch in a long time, only to hear a voice say, 'Time to turn around, Mister,' and then feeling a heavy hand fall on his shoulder and grip it tightly, immobilizing him.

Jail was an unlikely threat though. What they wanted out of him was a *mea culpa*, a satisfaction he would not give them. So what if he had minimised the extent to which he had fraternized with communist sympathizers in his youth? Of what significance was this misrepresentation, other than that it amounted to a betrayal of friendships he had cherished? If he had betrayed anyone, it was friends who had mattered enormously to him.

And now he was becoming a political liability to Pearson – that was clear.

He really did need to talk to someone unreservedly. The way he used to talk with Cornford, who would have understood that suicide can sometimes be an honourable action.

The wind must have intensified, its hissing not unlike that of a whistling kettle. The shutters shook continuously. The ambassador sat back, removed his glasses and placed them in a drawer. He rubbed his eyes and, with his right index finger, began tracing shapes in the new layer of dust that had settled on his desktop.

They say that after a *khamaseen* is over, the air smells wonderfully fresh and the sky is a clear blue.

Adel was eager to have his first real meeting with the ambassador. Everyone in the embassy had said he was a good man as well as very smart, smarter than most diplomats. Carrying the ambassador's customary mid-morning cup of tea on a tray, Adel discreetly knocked on the office door. If he could string a few words of English together that he'd memorised for the occasion, he would invite the ambassador to attend his wedding in Aswan in autumn. If that went well – and the receptionist had assured him it would – he might be so bold as to ask him what he thought of Nasser, an Alexandrian by birth who was succeeding in winning the approbation of Upper Egyptians, Nubians included, which was by no means a small feat.

'The ambassador might be resting so if he doesn't answer, walk quietly into his office and leave his cup of tea on the desk,' had been the secretary's instructions. It seemed rude to Adel to walk into the office uninvited, so he knocked once more. When he again received no answer, he reluctantly turned the door knob, half-opened the door and peeked inside the room.

The ambassador was lying on the couch with his shoes on and with his back to the door, apparently sleeping.

'He should be sleeping facing the door,' was Adel's immediate thought. A man sleeping with his back to a door conjured up disquieting images of defencelessness. Adel was tempted to turn back. When a man is resting, it is best not to disturb him, was a rule his father had taught him at a young age. But the secretary had been clear: he should leave the tea on the desk.

Adel tiptoed into the room and set the already-sweetened cup of tea on the desk. He was about to cover the cup with its saucer to keep the tea warm and the dust out when, from across the room a 'thank you' – first in English and then in heavily accented Arabic – startled him. Turning around, he saw an ambassador who did not look like one.

Now sitting on the couch's edge with his head down, hands pressing against his temples, this man seemed to be in pain. 'He must have a headache,' Adel assumed, and swiftly suggested in English, 'Sir, tea now? Tea good, very good.' He switched to Arabic and continued, '*Khamaseens* often cause headaches,' and pointed to his own head, even though the ambassador had yet to look up.

The ambassador raised his head and squinted. In the darkness of his office and without his glasses, he could barely see Adel. He liked the young man's voice; it was both cheerful and poised.

Adel stood erect next to the desk. Although he had met the ambassador a week earlier, he thought it fitting to reintroduce himself. 'My name is Adel,' he said in English.

'Adel,' the ambassador repeated, slowly rising to his feet. Appreciating the tactful reminder even though he did remember the name, the ambassador put on a ghost of a smile then walked towards his desk. To Adel, the ambassador seemed huge and old. To the ambassador, Adel seemed very slight and very young. Adel reached for the tea cup. 'Not now, not now,' the ambassador said.

'I'll drink it in a little while. First, I must find my glasses.' Adel remained by the desk, thinking of how he might mention his wedding to the ambassador without appearing presumptuous. He would leave his question about Nasser for another time. Today was not the right day for it.

The ambassador was now also standing by the desk, his fingers nervously thrumming against it. Not wanting to be left alone, he was trying hard to come up with a subject – any subject – that could become a topic of conversation, one that could be conducted more with gestures than words.

The *khamaseen* must have eased, for the shutters had stopped vibrating. 'Take me to the roof,' he suddenly instructed Adel in English, making sure to articulate each word as clearly as he could. 'To the roof!' he said again as he grabbed his glasses.

'Excuse me, sir, my English is very limited,' Adel said slowly in Arabic.

With the help of a dictionary, the ambassador translated his request to the bewildered Adel, who counselled that, with a *khamaseen* blowing, it was not such a good idea. In the end, however, he had no choice but to accede to the ambassador's firm request. From their limited exchange, he concluded that the ambassador's interest in going to the roof lay in a desire to look at the city shrouded in a *khamaseen*.

The wind had stopped blowing by the time they reached the roof, but dust still filled the air. You could smell it. It tickled inside your throat and nose. Adel stood behind the ambassador, who appeared lost in thoughts as he gazed out across the city. When he finally moved, he almost ran to the roof's outer edge and bent low over it, giving Adel a fright. Doing his best to keep his voice down, for it would be unseemly to shout at an ambassador, Adel cried out, 'Mister, mister!' before remembering to use the more formal but equally cautionary, 'Sir, sir!'

The ambassador straightened up and turned to face Adel, haltingly saying, 'I'm sorry. I didn't mean to frighten you.' He was not sure that Adel had understood him since he had apologised in English, so he struggled to remember the word for 'sorry' in Arabic. It was a simple word, but he couldn't think of it. The older man looked so contrite that Adel decided to lighten the atmosphere by extending his wedding invitation. The words he had committed to memory came rolling out of his mouth. 'My wedding in Aswan in September. We very happy if you and madam come to wedding.'

The ambassador smiled and nodded. 'Yes, of course we will come, it will be our pleasure. Attending a wedding is a wonderful way to get to know a country. Thank you very much for inviting us, Adel.' The two men stood next to each other in silence until the ambassador said, 'I'll look down the roof one more time, and then we can go back in.' Adel frowned and seemed about to say something, but the ambassador, more slowly this time, was already heading towards the roof's outer edge. Once there, he walked its whole length twice before pausing at a corner. Out of nowhere, a mouse came scurrying along, stopping near him. Adel hissed to chase the mouse away. The mouse stayed put. Adel hissed again but the mouse would not budge.

The ambassador seemed neither to notice the mouse nor to hear the hissing. His gaze had dropped from the horizon to the street below. As he leaned, he had the presentiment that what had started as a possibility would become reality: he would kill himself. For a brief moment, that idea brought him the relief he had been seeking for days. He stopped thinking of the accusations thrown at him. As if something had suddenly caught his interest, he leaned further down. A hand resting on his shoulder coupled with an urgent 'No sir, no!' brought back all the wretched thoughts. Patting his back, Adel soothingly repeated, '*Ma'alesh, ma'alesh*. All good, all good,' before switching to, 'You good man. Very good man. Very, very good man.' Without turning around, the ambassador whispered 'thank you' several times.

Back in the office, Adel offered to bring him a fresh cup of tea. The ambassador replied, 'Later perhaps, not now.' His eyes drifted towards the couch, but he said nothing to Adel about moving it out of the office.

Adel guessed that the ambassador would lie down again and go back to thinking whatever disturbing, devilish thoughts were driving him over the edge. Now was not the time to be leaving him alone. So ignoring propriety by remaining in the room, Adel asked the ambassador, 'Sir, what you think of revolution? What you think of Nasser? Is Nasser good man?'

Lee is Coming

Only three more steps before the landing, and then he could rest. Now only two. One. Finally, the landing. Bathed in perspiration, Aziz unfastened his shirt's top button. He had made it to the fifth floor. The bench he was hoping to sit on to catch his breath, the very same bench he used to climb on as a child, had vanished. There in the morning, gone by the afternoon. Leaning against the wall, he muttered, 'Stairs are good for me,' though he no longer believed it.

One more flight of stairs and he would be home.

Wafting up from the building's internal courtyard through a broken window came the smell of rotting garbage. He tried to breathe through his mouth, looking down at the floor and away from the shattered windowpane. His eyes fell on two dead cockroaches, the size of large dates. The sight of a few more cockroaches and he risked losing his love of dates! He looked up at the ceiling. Was that dangling, burnt-out light bulb in danger of falling down?

There were days when he accepted the building's state of disrepair and his own decline. Today was not such a day.

Five years had passed since, after a winter of losing game after game, he had given up playing squash. In his mind, he had entered old age that winter. He still swam, but only in a pool. Long gone were his days of braving sky-high waves and treacherous currents. 'You'll die, you fool!' his father used to shout at him, an admonishment that fortified his resolve to ignore not merely the red flag warning swimmers not to venture too far from shore, but often the black one enjoining them to stay out of the water altogether. The funny thing was that his father, himself a fearless swimmer, would then brag about having played Russian roulette with the sea in his youth.

The Mediterranean was one of the reasons he had moved from Cairo to Alexandria. He never tired of looking at it. The other reason was his reckoning that, in Alexandria, it would be easier for him to adjust to a life of counting piasters and his reduced means.

With his legs wobbly and his right knee throbbing, Aziz slowly climbed the last flight of stairs. He never begrudged the generous tips he gave the *bawab*, despite the dent they put in his ever-shrinking budget. Thanks to them, the landing on his floor was well lit and the cleanest in the building.

Before ringing the bell – one of his habits was to announce his arrival rather than to let himself in – Aziz took a handkerchief out of his pocket to wipe the sweat off his brow and the back of his neck. He also scrubbed at the palm of his right hand, which was black from the banister he had rested on during his climb upstairs.

He ran his tongue over his lips. They were dry and felt odd. The barber had gotten carried away and over-trimmed his moustache, baring the contours of his mouth. Aziz had forgotten how much like his mother's his mouth looked. He would rather not have been reminded. An old man has no wish to look like his mother; neither does a young one, for that matter.

They had been discussing Nasser when the barber attacked his moustache. It seemed that wherever he went these days, the subject of Nasser cropped up and people confided in him their thoughts – good and bad – about the president. People trusted that he would keep the tenor of the conversation to himself. Although he personified the ancien regime, he came across as capable of assessing both the past and the present objectively. He was not amongst those who spoke of yesterday as though it had been infinitely better than today. While snipping his moustache, his barber had predicted that, soon enough, marriages between the sons and daughters of the rising class of military men and those of the old bourgeoisie would create a new world, not altogether dissimilar from the pre-revolutionary world. 'They're nationalizing this and nationalizing that; it's a revolution, there's no doubt about it, but socialism it's not,' the barber had whispered, even though the two of them were alone in the shop. The barber had continued, 'It's just rechannelling the money, and whether people like me will be better off for it remains to be seen. But I think that it's wrong that good, honourable people like you have been hit so hard. Some people deserved to be brought down to size, but many did not.'

Who was to say, though, that he had not deserved to be stripped of his assets and forced to live modestly? If pressed, he would not know how to argue that what had been taken from him was rightfully his.

After patting what was left of his moustache, Aziz ran his hand over his head. 'Little hair left there too, but that's not the barber's fault,' he murmured.

'Don't tell me you climbed the six flights of stairs,' Elda said reproachfully.

Neither confirming nor contradicting, Aziz Bey gave her a feeble smile.

'Did you really need to go to the barber today?' Elda continued, as she followed him to the living room. He slumped down on his favourite armchair, one which a rich acquaintance who had inexplicably escaped the new regime's reach kept offering to buy at a good price. But Aziz refused to part with his armchair.

The shutters were drawn. The room's half-darkness suited his mood. 'Please, don't bother opening the shutters,' he begged, for he feared that Elda might.

'I'll get you some lemonade,' she offered. 'I just finished making some the way you like it, lots of lemon, a few mint leaves and only a hint of sugar.' After a slight pause, she added, 'The way she liked it too.'

He nodded twice, 'Yes, she did like it with lots of lemon.' He added, 'That's sweet of you.'

Elda showed no signs of going to the kitchen. She stood in front of Aziz, watching him.

'You need to put your feet up,' she suggested, and brought him a stool.

'Don't worry, I'm fine,' he assured her, but he was thankful. His knee was sore, the pain sharper than it had been in months. 'Why now?' he fumed silently as he stretched his leg out. He closed his eyes and rested his head against the back of the armchair.

'What will Lee think? To see Aziz so diminished, bordering on poor as well as shrivelled and old-looking, reduced to being a nobody when the Aziz she had known was rich, handsome and robust, a man of importance?' Such were the thoughts whirling through Elda's mind – and, of course, 'What will Lee think of him being married to me?'

Elda decided to leave the lemonade for later and let Aziz rest.

Much had changed since Aziz had last seen Lee in London, where he had gone to grant her a divorce so that she could marry Penrose – that artist and collector, quite a philanderer apparently – with whom she had a child. Only fifteen years had passed, but it might as well have been a lifetime. Divorced from Lee, Aziz had re-married, marrying *her*, Elda, the housekeeper and Lee's companion on trips to Europe, trips which few husbands would have tolerated. Too good a husband? Too weak a husband? Too unconcerned a husband? A husband keen on persuading his free and footloose wife that Middle Eastern men could be broad-minded? Or just a clear-sighted husband who knew that his hold on his wife was tenuous and his one chance at keeping her was to let her go? At the time, this was how Elda had judged Aziz for giving his blessing to Lee's trips to Europe in pursuit of her pleasures – whatever those might be.

And that was what she still thought. Treated by Lee as a friend, she too had succumbed to Lee's charm. She had been both amused and bemused by Lee's daring, Lee's wit, Lee's ups and downs, by Lee wanting it all: security and adventure; love and freedom; closeness and distance; a home but no obligations, and by Lee wanting to be both woman and man, child and adult. What she knew of Lee's antics and indiscretions she had never deemed appropriate to disclose to Aziz. Mindful of Elda's delicate position as a chaperone, Lee had been considerate enough never to discuss her affairs with her. As for Aziz, neither needing nor expecting Elda to open his eyes, he had guessed that 'his troubled soul', as he once described Lee to her parents, was partying hard in Europe and perhaps even falling in love. Any particulars Elda might have provided would have proven unnecessary.

Aziz's light snore told Elda he was asleep. Once, he had remarked that a person who falls asleep in the presence of another must trust that person very much. She had shrugged off his remark at the time, treating it as something said for fun. Now, she frequently caught herself thinking that there was something beautiful and moving about a person falling asleep in one's presence; it could speak of love.

She decided to lie down on the couch opposite Aziz's armchair and wait for him to wake up. But first she walked quietly across the room to close the curtains, even though the shutters were keeping the light out. He liked complete darkness when he napped. Curiously, light did not bother him as much at night.

'You'll need my pension,' he had said. 'I'd like you to have it and everything else too, which isn't much regrettably.' And then, 'We should get married, don't you think?'

She ought to have been elated but instead Elda had felt tearful. He had not said, 'I love you.' How absurd of her to have expected such a declaration from a man twice married to women regarded as amongst the most beautiful women of their era: Nimet and then Lee who, in addition to being beautiful, had the capacity as well as the temerity to live life on her own terms. Elda believed that Aziz's love of Lee had been, to a large extent, love of that rare and enviable and, at the same time, maddening quality.

'How was Lee?' Elda had asked Aziz the day after his return from England, fifteen years earlier. He had replied cryptically, 'It was Lee, but not Lee.' Elda had not dared probe further, although she could not imagine Lee not being Lee.

She would find out tomorrow what he had meant, as Lee was coming for lunch. It was Lee's first visit to Egypt since she had left the country, not knowing whether it would be for a few months or for good.

As soon as she lay down on the couch, Elda could tell that she would be unable to rest. She sat up and grabbed her knitting from a nearby basket. Knitting in the dark was as easy for her as knitting in broad daylight. Tonight, she should be able to finish the scarf, her modest present to Lee.

Was it being a mother that had changed Lee in some mysterious way? What she had witnessed in the war? Or, as some people said, maybe it was not knowing what to do with herself once the war was over.

'Lee's in Egypt. She'll be coming to Alex in a few days,' Aziz had told her earlier in the week.

Taken aback, Elda had exclaimed, 'But you didn't tell me she was coming to Egypt!' The 'why' that was at the tip of her tongue remaining unuttered.

'I wasn't sure she'd be coming. She left it a bit vague,' he had answered.

Was he just trying to placate her, or was it true? 'What brings her here now?' she had asked.

He had shrugged and said, 'She'll tell us.'

Gratified to hear him say 'us', Elda had nevertheless felt like a cheat, a fraud, an imposter, as though Lee could never lose her entitlement to being Aziz's wife.

'Perhaps she came to say goodbye to Egypt,' Elda had suggested.

'Perhaps, although it wouldn't be her style,' he had remarked. 'Lee was never sentimental.'

'And to see you, of course,' Elda had stated, her eyes unusually focused on her knitting.

He had remained silent.

She was still knitting when he woke up from his nap. 'Working hard at it,' he commented. 'Lee will be touched.'

'I hope she likes it, I'm not sure whether she likes mauve anymore. Colours that suit us when we're young may not suit us when we age. Lee must still be very beautiful.'

He did not take the bait, just quipped, 'And I'm still handsome.'

Elda said, 'She was very beautiful.'

'She was,' he agreed.

'What sort of mother do you think she is?' Elda asked. That was safer territory – or was it? He had very much wanted a child, and Lee had refused to have one. Too late, however, to change the subject.

'Probably the kind a child appreciates in retrospect,' he answered.

She laughed and gathered her courage to ask, 'And what sort of wife?' They had never discussed Lee before. 'A complicated wife?' she volunteered.

'It's been so long. I don't know whether what I think now is what I thought then,' he began by saying. He then carefully tried to explain, perhaps as much to himself as to her, 'She wasn't at all what one expects a wife to be like. That was part of her charm. She was the kind of wife that made it hard for another one to come into your life.' It was not a fair thing to be saying to Elda, but it was too late for him to retract his statement.

'I imagine so,' she said, seeming unperturbed.

Apologetic, Aziz said, 'How about your nice lemonade? I shall get us some.'

'Wait,' she said as she put down her knitting, 'I need to ask you something, I want to know what Lee thinks of us being married.'

'It doesn't matter,' he said. 'Besides, I'm sure she approves.'

'She said nothing about it in her letters?' Elda prodded. 'Nothing at all?'

'Her letters were short. She can write beautifully, but she never much liked letter-writing,' he said. 'Can I get the lemonade? I am very thirsty.' He got up gingerly and was relieved to find that his knee was better.

Elda watched him go to the kitchen, slightly limping. Once he was out of earshot, she uttered, 'It's strange that she's coming now.'

He came back carrying two glasses of lemonade which, after a sip, he pronounced excellent. 'The mint leaves really make a difference,' he stated. 'I wonder why people don't always make lemonade this way.' Then he asked, 'So what do you have in mind for lunch tomorrow? Do you need me to do any shopping in the morning? It's too bad that Zeinab won't be here to help you.' Elda was inspecting the scarf. 'It's all right. I'll manage. I'll prepare a fish meal,' she answered. 'I have a new recipe, with olives and peppers. I've got all the ingredients and I'll pick up the fish early in the morning. And for dessert, we'll have some *mehallabeyah*, without rose water though. Lee liked it without.'

'No one prepares fish as well as you do! She'll want your recipe. Apparently, she's into her cooking.'

'Into cooking?' Elda repeated, as though she had misheard.

'Yes, it's her new hobby. Well, more than a hobby, a new passion, so she says.'

'But I thought that she didn't say much in her letters,' Elda said, looking up from the scarf.

'She mentioned a couple of things, her love of cooking was one of them.'

'It's not something I'd have expected. Could it be the result of seeing death and starvation during the war?' Elda wondered aloud, before stating, 'Food is life.'

'It's very possible,' Aziz said.

'It must have something to do with the war,' Elda reiterated, shaking her head as if to say, 'Hard to believe that cooking has become Lee's new passion.'

Aziz opened the curtains, the shutters, and the balcony door. A refreshing breeze blew through the room. It would be a while before the sun set. He stepped on the balcony, from where he could both see and smell the sea. Lee coming tomorrow felt unreal. 'I'm counting on us talking at length,' she had written. Talking about what, though? How do you talk when the time is limited and there are years to bridge? When things that seemed to matter profoundly no longer do? She loved Penrose but was not happy, he could tell from the tone of her letter. On the eve of her departure from Egypt to join Penrose, he had told her that he would divorce her only if he could be sure that she had found the man who was going to make her truly happy.

It was a silly thing to have said – it was saying: 'Look at what a good sort I am.' Nimet, then Lee. Nimet was dead, some thought because of Lee. He was the culprit, if there was one. He had left one for the other who, in turn, would leave him. Best not to dwell on any of that, on Nimet killing herself years after he had divorced her, or on Lee, who had put away her camera in favour of pots and pans and was drinking too much. Did she even eat those fine dishes that had replaced her photos of life and death?

'You'll catch cold,' he heard Elda say. If only Elda knew how detached he felt from Lee. He wished he could feel a bit of pain, anger, or even some excitement about the coming visit, but he felt nothing of the kind, only that Lee's visit was disrupting his routine. Aziz went back in, sat down in his armchair, and reached for Saint Exupery's *Wind, Sand and Stars,* which lay on the side table. The older he got, the more fiction bored him. Only factual subjects, particularly geography, sustained his interest. He began reading while Elda, back to knitting, seemed to be studying the surrealist painting hanging above the mahogany sideboard across from her.

'I've never been able to figure this out,' she said all of a sudden. 'What's the meaning of this painting?'

Aziz looked up. 'What are you referring to?'

'The painting,' she said as though it should be self-evident which of the many pictures in the room she was talking about.

'Ah, the painting,' he said.

'There's blue sky or a blue sea, I'm not sure which, and sand. The white plank could be some sort of diving board.'

'The cup on top of it is clearly a cup,' Aziz chuckled.

'The reddish-brown liquid in it doesn't look particularly appetizing,' Elda said.

'It looks thick and sticky,' Aziz agreed.

'Now those wings that stick out of it are strange. They must be a bird's wings.'

Aziz nodded, 'Yes, a bird's wings, perhaps.'

'Did Penrose not want to give it a title, or could he not think of one?' Elda mused.

'Why don't you ask Lee tomorrow?' Aziz proposed, and went on to joke: 'A greedy bird drowning in a cup. That's it. Let's call it *Drowning Bird* and ask Lee what she thinks of that title.'

'What if she wants it? Will you give it to her?' Elda asked, not voicing the rest of her thought: 'You've given her more than enough.'

'I would, if she asks. He painted it for her, dedicated it to her, so it's hers.'

'Do you like it?' Elda asked.

'Not really,' he said. Could he be objective enough to judge a painting Penrose had done the summer Lee and Penrose had fallen in love? He looked at it only to reach the same conclusion he had reached when first seeing it: he honestly did not like it.

'If you don't like it, why hang it?' Elda asked.

'It reminds me of old times,' he answered. 'It's absurd. As absurd as my life was then.'

'Your life was not absurd,' Elda objected.

'Looking back, it seems to have been,' he said.

'No use looking back; it can be deceptive,' Elda said, thinking that Lee was one of those people who assume that they are entitled to whatever they happen to fancy.

'Lee was not meant to be a wife,' Aziz let out. 'She's been drowning in her marriage to Penrose, trying to be a wife.'

'Maybe she's not quite as unhappy as you believe her to be,' Elda responded, more forcefully than she meant to.

'I hope you're right,' he said. 'I wanted her to be happy, very much so.' Then he asked, 'So what's for dinner tonight?'

***

The doorbell rang just as Elda began tossing a big green salad with plenty of cucumber. The potato dish – one layer of potatoes, one of onions and one of tomatoes – was baking in the oven, as was the sea bass over which she would be pouring a spicy tomato sauce just before serving it. The *mehallebeyah* was ready and in the fridge. Instead of pistachios or almonds, which were hard to find and prohibitively expensive, Elda had used peanuts to garnish it; remembering that Lee liked cardamom, she had added a generous amount of that too.

When the doorbell rang, she rushed to close the kitchen door and returned to the salad, tasting it and tossing it. Not enough lemon, nor enough salt; too much mustard, perhaps a touch of sugar, or, better yet, honey, how about some pepper, and dill of course, as well as raisins… she probably should have mixed in some shredded carrots or radishes to add a touch of colour, but it was too late for that, or was it? She could hear footsteps and voices drawing near, Lee's voice, Lee saying, 'Let's first go and see Elda. I'll have a drink later.'

Elda stopped tossing the salad and though she would have rather hidden somewhere, she resolutely walked towards the door, her cheeks burning. She opened the door and there, her arms wide-open, stood plain-looking Lee.

'Lee!' exclaimed Elda. Of the two women, she – Elda – was now by far the better-looking one. She was unprepared for that and almost felt guilty as well as vaguely disappointed.

Lee and Elda hugged and then, saying that the kitchen smelled divine, Lee hurried over to see what was cooking and half-opened the oven door.

'Not fair, this is *my* kitchen,' Elda would have liked to
object.

Standing by the door, Aziz smiled at Elda as their eyes
met.

Still admiring the potato dish, Lee asked, 'How is it, to live in
this new Egypt?'

Café Astra

'Say it,' Ramzi ordered his brother as he pinned him to the floor.

'Move first – then I'll say it,' Marwan shouted, struggling to sit up.

'I want to hear those words now,' Ramzi demanded.

'I'm suffocating!'

'It can't be that bad – you're screaming, you're moving.'

'You're really hurting me,' Marwan protested. Ramzi was now lying on top of him, their faces almost touching.

'I'm in no hurry. I'll wait. I'm not getting up until I hear those words.'

'Shouldn't you be studying?' Marwan tried. 'If you're going to apply to the military academy, you should be improving your grades.'

'Shut up!' Ramzi snapped, sitting up a little. 'It's not as if you're doing so brilliantly at school yourself.'

'But I've no great ambitions, whereas you do,' Marwan said.

'It's time you start thinking of how to become a movie director instead of just dreaming about it – that's if you're serious at all. Dreams are good up to a point. Now, let me hear you say 'I am no match for your superior strength.'

'But since we both know that to be the case, why do you want to hear me say it?' Marwan asked.

'You're not talking yourself out of this. I'm not getting up.'

'Please, tell me what you'll get out of hearing me say that I'm not as strong as you are. I don't understand!' Marwan said.

Ramzi made no reply. Sensing that he had scored a point, Marwan was ready to comply with his older brother's stupid request. 'I am no match for your superior strength, mister. You're infinitely stronger than I am,' he began, and then carried on, 'You're as strong as an ox, as strong as a bull, as strong as a rhinoceros, as strong a bear, as strong as a hippopotamus, as strong as...'

'Enough, enough!' Ramzi interrupted, but he did get off his brother.

Marwan remained on the floor.

'Are you planning to spend the rest of your afternoon on the floor?' Ramzi asked, tucking his shirt back into his trousers. Then, in a tone far too casual to be natural, he asked, 'So what do you think of Esmeralda? Do you think she's pretty?'

'Yes, she is pretty, very pretty,' Marwan said.

'You stay away from her. Understood?'

'What are you thinking? That I'm going to chase after the girl you're in love with? What's going on with you? Are you going a bit crazy because it's getting close to exam time?'

'I'm just warning you! She's a sweet and decent girl.'

'Who said otherwise? Look, I told you she was pretty because I know you're in love with her. If I'd said "I don't think she's pretty", you'd have been disappointed, even mad at me. I can't win.'

Ramzi grabbed his brother's hands and pulled him up. 'Only two more weeks before the exams,' he complained. 'My heart's not in it. I can't focus. How can I, with what's going on?'

'Do you think there's going to be a war?' Marwan asked, as they sat down in their bedroom.

'I do! So does Uncle Taha! And so does our chief-of-staff, Amer. Apparently, Amer thinks that war is inevitable, that if we don't strike first, Israel will. Uncle Taha can't understand why Nasser is dithering.'

'Is it true then that Nasser and Amer don't see eye to eye?'

'Absolutely! Didn't you hear what Uncle Taha was saying last week? What were you dreaming of? Movie-making?'

'Nasser and Amer have been friends for years – they wouldn't have a major falling out,' Marwan put forward.

'I wouldn't be so sure. According to Uncle Taha, many officers prefer Amer to Nasser. They're friends, but they're also rivals.'

'I remember Uncle Taha saying Amer panicked during the 1956 war and was criticised by Nasser for urging surrender.' Marwan then suggested, 'That could be the reason he's acting tough now, if it's true that he's in favour of us striking first.'

'There's no "if"! Uncle Taha knows what he's talking about. His sources are reliable.'

'I think Mother's back.'

'Not one word about Esmeralda to her,' Ramzi warned Marwan.

'You treat me as if I'm a child. Have you forgotten I'll be sixteen in a few days?'

'How *can* I forget, since you keep reminding us! Relax, you'll get presents.'

'Give me a hint,' Marwan begged.

'You're as impatient as a child,' Ramzi laughed. 'By the way, what do you think of these trousers? They're new.'

'You look like James Bond.'

'Don't butter me up. It won't get you more presents,' Ramzi said.

Nobody would have guessed that Ramzi and Marwan were brothers. On the short side, seventeen-year-old Ramzi was robust and swarthy, with coarse hair as jet black as his eyes. With a slighter build and not quite sixteen, Marwan was fair and already taller than his brother. His eyes and hair were the colour of honey. His mother liked to tease him by saying that he seemed forever astonished at the world. The shape of his eyebrows gave him that quizzical expression.

In 1948, their father had fought in Falluja alongside Nasser. He survived the war only to die of a heart attack seven years later. Sometimes Ramzi told his friends that his father died during the war. Not daring to contradict his brother in public, Marwan would object privately to that lie and Ramzi would always argue the same thing, 'Why nit-pick? He *could* have died during the war. Didn't Mother tell us about his near misses on the frontline? As an aspiring movie director, you should begin to consider facts in a more imaginative way.'

'I was hoping to find you buried in your books,' the boys' mother said as she walked into their room. The boys smiled sheepishly. They adored their mother, who was young and beautiful. After their father's death, rejecting her brother's advice that they would benefit from a paternal presence, she had refused to remarry. Her brother, their Uncle Taha, had concluded that she enjoyed being in charge of the boys and of her affairs. He was right. She knew how to handle her sons and proved to have good money sense. With the little money left by her husband, she had started a business, which she ran from a second apartment in the same building they lived in. She bought small pieces of furniture and *objets d'art* from families leaving Egypt and sold them to foreigners, mostly diplomats, as well as to the few Egyptians who could afford them. Even though times were hard, her business was lucrative; she had good taste and little competition. To keep an eye on her sons, all she needed to do was run up two flights of stairs. It was a perfect arrangement.

'Your Uncle Taha called to say that Nasser may have come to the conclusion that war is unavoidable,' the boys' mother reported.

'He said this over the phone? Even though he's been warning us not to speak about politics over the phone because they're tapped?' Marwan said.

'Well, he was careful. He didn't quite spell it out, but I got the message,' his mother explained.

'Nasser is finally seeing the light!' Ramzi trumpeted. 'Good!'

'*Is* it good?' his mother challenged him. 'He must have had his reasons not to want to start a war in the first place.'

'Such as?' Ramzi asked.

'That we're not prepared, or not as well prepared as we should be,' she speculated.

'Don't even think that!' Ramzi urged his mother.

'There's something I've never understood,' interjected Marwan. 'If Nasser didn't want a war, why did he ask the peacekeepers to leave the Sinai, and why did he block the Straits of Tiran?'

'Politics and war are not your strong subjects,' Ramzi threw at him.

Ignoring his brother, Marwan hazarded, 'Maybe both Nasser and Amer are bluffing; maybe neither one of them really wants a war.'

'You're full of ideas today. Perhaps good material for movies, although I'm not even sure about that,' Ramzi said.

'I want you boys to go back to your studying. The crisis is no excuse for you to put your books away. You in particular, Ramzi, can't afford to do poorly.'

'Don't worry, Mother!' Ramzi said and gave her a military salute.

'How can I not?' their mother sighed as she left to return to her shop.

As soon as he heard the apartment door close behind her, Ramzi exclaimed, 'Mothers!' and shook his head. 'So you like my trousers,' he grinned. 'By the way, before I forget to tell you, remember what you had asked me to do on your behalf? It's done!'

'What I asked you to do?' Marwan wondered, looking perplexed. Then he blushed. 'You don't mean to say that you took it seriously?'

'Of course I did. What are brothers for?'

Mortified to feel his cheeks burning crimson, Marwan became even redder.

'Take it easy, you seem to be on fire,' Ramzi said. 'It's all set for next Thursday afternoon. You go to Astra. She'll be there. She'll recognise you. I described you to her.'

'You mean Astra, the café on Tahrir?'

'What other Astra is there?' Ramzi said irritably before answering, more gently, 'Yes, Astra on Tahrir. That's where she usually goes.'

'I don't know, *ya* Ramzi. I don't know,' Marwan said.

'You asked me to do you a favour, I deliver and suddenly you're all in a knot,' Ramzi pointed out.

'I wasn't really serious,' Marwan tried to explain.

'I took you seriously.'

Marwan ran his fingers through his hair. 'Is she attractive?' he asked.

'She is attractive, although I cannot guarantee that she's your type, I have a feeling she might be.'

'I'll think about it,' Marwan said.

'Suit yourself. I'm not pushing you. It doesn't matter to me. If you decide to stay at home and read a book instead, or go to the movies, I won't hold it against you.'

Marwan nodded and smiled at his brother, who could be a big brute but loved him. Up until only a couple of years earlier, Ramzi's persistent bullying, never too terrible but nevertheless annoying, used to make him wonder whether his brother liked him at all. Then came the day when, emulating Ramzi, Marwan had entered their fifth-floor apartment by inching along the narrow outside ledge that ran from beneath a nearby window to their dining room balcony. Seeing his younger brother suddenly appear on the balcony, Ramzi, who happened to be in the dining room, had turned white as a shroud. Instead of heaping praise on Marwan, he had showered him with insults, threatening him with a real beating, were he ever to catch him doing it again. 'You may be an idiot of a brother, but I would rather have you alive than dead,' Ramzi had shouted. After much yelling from both sides, the two brothers had calmed down and promised each other never to set foot on the ledge again. For Marwan, it was an easy promise to make since he had no intention of repeating the experience. He had been scared stiff on that ledge.

On June the fourth, Marwan's aunts, uncles and cousins had been invited for a celebratory dinner. Though it was his birthday, the likelihood that war would break out was the principal subject of conversation before, during and after dinner. The previous day Nasser had given an interview with a British journalist, offering assurances that there would be no escalation of tensions on the part of Egypt, which was about to send an envoy to Washington to negotiate a compromise solution. A mere few hours after that interview, Nasser had declared that he expected Israel to attack from the air within days. Everybody at the dinner table agreed that it was difficult to know what conclusions to draw from these declarations.

Later that night, as they were getting ready to go to bed, Ramzi asked Marwan, 'So have you made up your mind about tomorrow? Will you be going to Astra?'

'Maybe,' Marwan replied without revealing that Café Astra and the girl Ramzi had arranged for him to meet had been on his mind all day long. 'What sort of men frequent that cafe?' he inquired.

'Mostly dreamers, so you should feel at home there,' his brother teased.

To change the subject, Marwan asked, 'Where's my present?'

'At Astra,' Ramzi said with a laugh, while at the same time handing him a heavy book inscribed, 'To Marwan, future movie maker whose name will for sure appear in some such book one day. He might even get a whole paragraph.' It was a history of cinema.

Marwan was tempted to give his brother a hug, but it was not quite Ramzi's style. Instead, he asked him how things were going with Esmeralda.

Glumly, Ramzi answered. 'Her parents have decided to emigrate. The first I heard was yesterday. She didn't tell me earlier because she was hoping they wouldn't get visas, but they did. They'll be going to the US.'

'When?' exclaimed Marwan, stunned.

'I'm not sure. Within the next six months is my guess. And if there is a war, they might go sooner.' For a moment, Ramzi looked disconsolate; however, he quickly pulled himself together by throwing a pillow at his brother and singing: 'Happy birthday to you, you handsome one.' Then, looking serious again, he stated, 'Esmeralda will come back when we get married. She will wait for me; she said she would.'

'I'm sure she will,' Marwan agreed, even though he was thinking that, of the two of them, Ramzi was the real dreamer.

In the early morning hours of June the fifth, an Israeli armada of fighter-bombers destroyed much of Egypt's Air Force. It was the beginning of a military debacle the extent of which became clear to Egyptians only some days later; at first they were told they were winning the war. Only those listening to foreign radio stations knew Egypt was losing – badly. Ramzi and Marwan were not amongst those in the know. They whiled away the first two days of the war, endlessly discussing what Egypt would do once victory was proclaimed. Every now and then, Ramzi would mention the rendezvous he had arranged for Marwan at Astra, judging it to be perfect timing – the rendezvous would be in keeping with the jubilant mood bound to be sweeping the nation. Non-committal, Marwan would smile, giving no hints of his intentions.

On June the eighth, their mother woke them up with disturbing news. Their Uncle Taha had dropped by first thing in the morning to say that Nasser and Amer had had a huge shouting match over the conduct of the war; things were not going so well.

'How does he know?' Ramzi roared.

'You yourself said that his sources were reliable and that he has many friends in the army,' Marwan noted.

'I didn't ask you, I asked Mother,' Ramzi barked at him.

'Stop bickering!' their mother enjoined them. 'Nasser is bound to be giving a speech any time now – he can't leave us on tenterhooks for much longer. I'm staying home today,' she announced.

No sooner had their mother left the room than the phone rang. Ramzi's best friend, whose aunt was a school teacher, wanted to let them know that school exams were being postponed indefinitely.

In the evening, Uncle Taha called on them again. Ramzi greeted him with a barrage of questions.

'Israel apparently controls the Sinai,' his Uncle Taha began, but before he could elaborate, Ramzi had fled to his room and slammed the door behind him.

'Let him be. Don't make a fuss about this,' Taha advised his sister. 'He's taking it very hard, as I'd expect him to.' To Marwan, he said, 'I can't help but think of how upset your father would be to see Israel victorious again. Tomorrow might bring better news. We must keep hoping.'

Marwan couldn't sleep that night. His head was bursting with dread, confusion, and desire. He would have liked to talk to Ramzi – to talk about their father, the war, Esmeralda and the rendezvous scheduled for the following day at Astra. But lying on top of his bed with his clothes still on, Ramzi was sound asleep, and had been for hours. He hadn't stirred, even when Marwan had unlaced his shoes and taken them off his feet.

'How can I be thinking of such a thing, today of all days?' Marwan asked himself as he lay in bed, staring at the ceiling. He was unable to shake off his disappointment at the prospect of missing the rendezvous at the café. Now that events were taking the matter out of his hands – the whole country could be upside down by tomorrow – all his hesitations had evaporated; he was aching to go. Had Ramzi truly arranged for him to meet that girl? And was it in the afternoon or the evening that she was supposed to be there? He wasn't certain anymore. Surely though, she too was bound to skip the rendezvous. 'It wasn't meant to be,' Marwan whispered, and sought to console himself with the prospect that maybe in Alex this summer... but *would* they be holidaying in Alex this summer?

To put that whole business out of his mind, he turned his thoughts to Ramzi, to how bereft his brother would feel after Esmeralda's departure. So, Ramzi had sensed that he too was smitten by Esmeralda. Naturally, he would never do anything about it. Esmeralda was totally off limits; she was Ramzi's love. Might the girl he was supposed to meet at Astra look at all like

Esmeralda? What was her name? How much money or what gift, if any, would she be expecting? He hadn't asked and Ramzi hadn't told him. Maybe that rendezvous was humbug and his brother had been pulling his leg. It probably was a practical joke. Or was it?

In the morning, their mother greeted them with the announcement that Nasser would be giving a speech in the evening. Ramzi spent much of the day in his bedroom while, loafing on the balcony, Marwan was leafing through his book on the history of cinema. Their mother hardly put the phone down the whole day. The three of them skipped lunch.

In the evening, neighbours joined them to watch Nasser deliver his speech. If the news was bad, best to hear it with others, to make it more bearable.

'I have taken a decision with which I need your help. I have decided to withdraw totally and for good from any official post or political role and to return to the ranks of the masses, performing my duty in their midst, like any other citizen,' their grim-faced leader informed them.

The instant the speech ended, Ramzi rushed to his room, re-emerging seconds later to shout, 'I'm going out,' as he dashed towards the door. 'Wait for me,' Marwan cried. Before their mother could object, the two boys were out in the street, running down Soliman Pasha Street towards Midan el Tahrir. They were not alone.

Rushing towards the Midan from all sides, men, women and children were howling 'God protect us' and 'Don't leave us, ya Nasser!'

Halfway to the Midan, Marwan panted, 'What do we do once we get to Tahrir?' Ramzi did not answer.

It was dark. Their voices were beginning to grow hoarse from chanting with the crowd that filled the entire Midan 'Lead us ya, Nasser! Don't leave us!' 'We shall fight!' and 'We are your soldiers!'

Not far behind them was Café Astra. 'I'll be back,' Marwan suddenly said to Ramzi. To reach the café, Marwan had to elbow his way through the growing crowd. Right in front of Astra's front window, four women wearing rather tight, short dresses were standing close to one another. Marwan's eyes were immediately drawn to them. He reckoned that they were between twenty and twenty-five. The four women were chanting along with everyone else. The one who seemed to be the oldest was crying; the woman next to her had her arm wrapped around her shoulder.

Which one is she? Marwan wondered. Just then, the smallest and youngest woman looked his way. Even though clingy, her black dress was tasteful, he decided. She reminded him ever so slightly of Esmeralda. He could feel himself blushing and averted his eyes. When he risked glancing at the women again, she was staring at him and had stopped chanting. It seemed to him that she was smiling at him with her eyes. Would it be crazy for him to try to squeeze into the jam-packed café and to expect her to follow him there? If she did, they could reschedule their rendezvous.

By now, he was certain that she was the girl – she did look more like a girl than a woman – the girl Ramzi had arranged for him to meet. With the slightest tilt of the head, Marwan signalled to her that he was going into the café. He managed to thread his way to the counter. On an impulse, he ordered five lemonades, even though he had no idea how he would carry them. Maybe with the girl's help?

But after placing his order, he remembered that he had left his wallet at home. The cashier told him not to worry; he could come back and pay if Nasser rescinded his resignation, and if Nasser let his resignation stand, the country would go to the dogs so no amount of money would make a difference.

Turning round, a glass of lemonade in each hand, he came face to face with a livid Ramzi who grabbed him by the shoulders while screaming, 'Are you out of your mind? You're a complete child!'

Some of the lemonade slopped out of the glasses. Blinded by rage, Marwan slammed the glasses onto the counter; then he shoved his brother with such force that, were it not for a man who happened to be standing behind him, Ramzi would have fallen down.

'Calm down, you two,' the man rebuked them.

'Are you not aware of the catastrophe that has befallen us?' another man threw in.

'This isn't the time to be having silly arguments,' the cashier said.

'Children!' cried the employee who had just prepared the lemonades.

Turning away from his brother, Ramzi silently made his way towards the door. Men stepped aside to let him pass.

Leaving the lemonades on the counter, Marwan hurried behind him, unsure whether he would apologise or ask for an apology.

Once outside Café Astra, Marwan took a quick look at the group of women. There were only three of them left. The youngest, the Esmeralda look-alike, was gone. As Ramzi disappeared into the crowd, Marwan approached the women. He stood beside them and resumed chanting 'Don't leave us, ya Nasser!' while trying in vain to choke back the tears streaming down his cheeks. The woman who had been crying earlier gave him a handkerchief and assured him it was clean.

Kissinger's Friend

'You're married to your work,' his father had fired. His mother had struck back, 'Better than being married to oneself, as *you* are.' At home, in bed with a nasty flu, he had overheard much of their heated exchange. Since that row, his parents hardly spoke to each other and studiously avoided each other. Almost a year had passed, and they had yet to make their peace. Like busy boarders in a hotel, they now used home mostly for sleeping, showering, making phone calls, and snacking in the kitchen.

Their rooms were at opposite ends of the apartment. Separate bathrooms and different schedules made it reasonably easy for them to cohabit without having to interact. She rose at dawn and went to bed not long after dusk; he came out of his room after eight and was rarely home before midnight.

Radwan had never taken sides with either of his parents. The rare times he let himself think of their relationship, he blamed them equally for being constantly on the warpath. They had been quarrelling or arguing – about everything and nothing – for as long as he could remember. On stumbling across photos of them affectionately holding hands in their youth, his immediate reaction had been, 'It can't be them – it must be my aunt and uncle.'

Why his mother and father had gotten married in the first place remained a mystery to him. It hadn't been an arranged marriage. There must have been love or some attraction between the athletic young man, a rising star in the military, and the bookish young woman planning to do a doctorate in psychology. The young man would become a respected general, and the young woman a child psychologist with a solid practice. At least marriage had not been in the way of their careers. Still, the partnering of these two had been a mismatch and now they were unwilling or unable to make a clean break. Even though he had succeeded in shielding himself from their frequent altercations – it was their lives, after all – it much relieved Radwan that they had finally found a way of living together without living together.

His work in the President's Bureau of Information kept him very busy. He had obtained the position through his friend Ali, rather than through his father's connections. Wanting to do right by his friend, he was giving it his all. He actually liked the work. Sifting through the press and government memos to unearth and piece together sensitive information required three attributes: patience, a systematic mind and a nose for what might turn out to be valuable data. Radwan was the perfect man for the job.

Though not outright disapproving, both his father and his mother were not too pleased with his being part of the president's entourage. Radwan was not surprised at their lack of enthusiasm. His mother continued to venerate Nasser despite his bitter defeat in 1967, regarding his successor with the utmost suspicion; in her eyes, no successor to Nasser could match the great man. As for his father, in the privacy of his home he made no bones about being unhappy with the president for undermining the military while strengthening the police force and the Interior Ministry. Since his so-called 'Corrective Revolution' and the arrest of officials conspiring against him, the president had been relying increasingly on this ministry for security purposes. The military was, therefore, losing some of its control over the domestic situation. When he began working for the Bureau, it had crossed Radwan's mind that his father might see some advantage in having a son with access to sensitive information, since it could prove useful to the army. Fortunately, his father had not put him to the test by asking him questions he could not answer. Were it not for his father being regarded as apolitical – therefore no threat to the president – Radwan would not have been hired for the job.

Ali, the trusted friend who had gotten Radwan his job, barged into his office with an air of urgency, immediately closed the door then stood next to it and cleared his throat. It was late in the evening, almost night time. Radwan was still sorting through the mass of fresh clippings piled up on his desk.

'What's up?' he asked Ali, sensing that something was brewing.

'Nothing, nothing,' said Ali unconvincingly, while he put his hand on the door handle as though he was about to leave.

'Sit down,' Radwan motioned towards the chair. 'You look like you want to say something.'

'Hardly anyone's around today,' Ali said.

'You didn't come to tell me *that*.'

Ali played with the door handle.

'Please sit down – you're making me nervous,' said Radwan.

'It's time to eat,' Ali announced.

'Don't you see the mountain of papers in front of me?'

'I do, I do, but let's go. Come on, let's go,' he beseeched Radwan. 'We can drive in my car – you can leave yours here overnight and I'll pick you up tomorrow morning.'

'Could Ali have finally fallen in love?' Radwan laughed and got up. 'Let's,' he said as he grabbed a light overcoat. He would need a heavier one soon. November was around the corner.

'Pigeon?' Ali asked, as he started the car.

'Sounds good to me,' Radwan acquiesced.

While he was driving, Ali neither spoke nor turned on the radio, which was unusual.

'He must be really smitten,' Radwan concluded.

At the restaurant, no sooner had they ordered than Ali asked Radwan if he could keep something strictly to himself.

'You know me, so judge for yourself,' Radwan replied.

Ali leaned over the table towards him and, although no one was anywhere near them, he whispered, 'You won't believe me but the big man is going to Israel. To Jerusalem.'

'The president in Israel?' Radwan whispered back. 'What are you saying? You're joking!'

'I'm not,' Ali murmured. 'It's going to happen. He's going to do it, even though everyone around him is trying to dissuade him. He'll have to deal with several resignations. But he'll do it. Trust me!'

'But why? Why go to Israel? Why does he need to do *that*?'

'That's exactly the question Fahmy and Gamassy have been asking him. They're dead set against this trip, but he won't listen. His mind's made up. I'm sure they'll quit, and he'll need new men to head foreign affairs and the army. Many changes are on the horizon.'

'I'm speechless. What do you think about it?'

Frowning, Ali paused before suggesting, 'Maybe it's time to do things differently. It's not as if we've achieved much since the 1948 War. Perhaps we need new ways of thinking; perhaps we need to show the world a different side of Egypt than what they're used to seeing.'

'So you agree with the president?' Radwan asked, astonished. Ali had always talked tough about how Israel should be dealt with and, behind closed doors, had often expressed his belief that in 1973 Egypt threw away its victory by fighting a limited war. Yet now, his friend seemed to be accepting the unimaginable, the unthinkable – an Egyptian president going to Israel.

'I don't know, I honestly don't know. But something good may come out of this. One can only hope.' Then, leaning forward, still speaking softly, his friend added, 'I may be going too.'

Thunderstruck, Radwan asked, 'To Jerusalem?'

Ali nodded.

'I don't know what to say.'

'It takes a while for that sort of thing to sink in. It's a big thing, very big.'

'Yes,' Radwan said. 'It's a big thing.'

'Mum's the word,' Ali said. 'You haven't heard anything, you know nothing.'

'No problem – it's so unbelievable that I already doubt I heard you properly,' Radwan promised.

'Best to assume I was talking wildly, as I often do,' Ali said, and they both laughed uneasily.

'Have I slept at all?' Radwan asked himself the following day. He had forgotten to close his shutters and draw the curtains that night. From his bed, he could see the morning light just beginning to appear in the sky. He could hear his parents talking in the kitchen, and though he couldn't quite make out what they were saying, at least they sounded calm.

What had happened? What sudden and unexpected harmony! Radwan was bewildered, though foremost on his mind was that Ali was picking him up this morning and might already be regretting having confided in him. It could be an awkward ride.

His mother's voice was rising in anger, 'Kissinger's friend!'

Radwan jumped out of bed and rushed to the kitchen where his parents, both in their dressing gowns, were sitting at the table, drinking tea and talking softly once more. They looked gloomy.

'What's new?' his father immediately asked him.

'Nothing. Just the usual,' Radwan responded.

'The usual?' his mother exclaimed. 'Egypt's president going to Israel is the usual?'

'Slowly, slowly,' his father urged his mother.

'What's the matter, Mother?' Radwan said, wondering with dread, *Will I be blamed for the news being out? If they know about it, others must know too.*

'*Ya* Radwan, "the matter" is what your Mother just said. You know what the matter is,' his father pressed him. 'Tell us what you know.'

'You probably know more than I do,' Radwan answered and stared at the kettle he had put on to boil.

His mother erupted, 'So you won't talk! You won't tell your parents what's happening, what this crazy president intends to do! What does the man think? That America and Israel will be overcome by his generosity? Hasn't he given them enough?

He expelled the Russian experts to please America; he met with Kissinger once, twice, got nothing out of him; he started a war, was winning it but then stopped to please his American friends and agreed to most of their terms; again, to please them, he lifted the food subsidies and ignored how that would affect the Egyptian people about whom he couldn't care less. Over and over he gives to his beloved Americans.' She shook her head. 'What for? Does he think this will buy him a place in heaven? What are we getting in return? He may be getting something, but what about his country? What about the Palestinians?' She took a deep breath: 'Speak!' she demanded.

His father must have been the bearer of the news. He would have loved to ask his father who in the army knew, but it would open up a conversation he couldn't have.

'You have strong views, you always have —,' he was interrupted by his father shouting, 'so you know about it and told us nothing?'

'I don't know what you're talking about,' Radwan replied, standing now in the middle of the kitchen with his cup of tea in hand.

'Radwan, listen to me. This is not the time to play dumb. Unlike you, I'll speak the truth. I'm disappointed in you. Very disappointed. You don't tell your father something as significant as this? What has gotten into you?'

Rage at his father's superior tone took hold of Radwan. His fingers clenched the cup tighter as, barely in control of his own tone, he told his father, 'I'm no longer a child, so please don't talk to me that way.'

'I knew that this job would go to his head,' his mother lamented. 'I was against his taking it, but I didn't want to interfere in his life.

I wish I had, though. I wish I'd disregarded all the theories about how you're supposed to deal with a grown-up child.'

'Let's get back to the more important subject,' his father said. 'What do you know about this trip to Israel *ya* Radwan? And what do you *think* about it?'

'I know nothing, I think nothing; it's not even seven in the morning. I'm being picked up soon and I haven't even showered,' Radwan said. Then out of his mouth slipped the words, 'Why always resist change, why not look at the world with fresh eyes?'

'Nonsense,' his father shouted. 'So you think that by going to Israel, "Kissinger's friend", as your mother rightly calls your president – although she could also call him, quite simply, America's *lackey* – will bring about positive change? Are you dreaming, or simply trying to protect your job? Let me tell you that nothing, *nothing* good whatsoever, will come out of that trip. Your president will end up giving a bit more of Egypt to Israel – that's all you can expect, and that's what you'll get. As for the Americans, wasn't it his dear Kissinger who said, "America doesn't pay for what's given freely?" And why should they pay, if we're willing to offer it to them on a silver platter?'

'I don't think there's any point in us discussing this. I have work to do, plenty of it. I must get ready to go.' Radwan put his cup of tea on the counter and left the kitchen.

'He's not my son.' Radwan stopped in the hallway. Had he just heard his father utter those words? Is this what his father had been thinking all along? Is this why his parents had been at loggerheads with each other all these years? Should he go back to the kitchen and ask them, point blank?

***

In the car, Ali made small talk. Halfway to work, he stopped the car. 'Let's stretch our legs a bit,' he suggested. Radwan guessed that his friend wanted to say something and thought it best to speak outside the car, fearing it might be bugged. They took a few steps and found themselves alone on the sidewalk. Ali lit a cigarette, forgetting to offer him one. 'Would *you* go to Jerusalem, if you were me?' he asked.

'Are you inviting me to come along?' Radwan asked.

Ali smiled.

'I'd consider it,' Radwan said, thinking, 'Why not? If they want me, I might just go. Things need to change.'

We Can Only Do So Much Dreaming

They hugged and kissed several times and then looked at each other, holding hands and shouting, '*mush ma'ul, mush ma'ul*' – 'unbelievable, unbelievable' – and hugging and kissing again; and now, in French, Arabic and English, interrupting each other, they shouted how happy they were to finally spend some time together. Nevine even had to wipe away a teardrop, for which Mona admonished her, saying, 'Now don't you start crying. It'll make me want to cry. We should be laughing, not crying!' Thereupon, the tears really began pouring out of Nevine's eyes. While wiping them with the back of one hand, she adjusted her hijab with the other.

Only then did it hit Mona that her friend was wearing a full hijab covering all her hair, not just a loosely tied scarf. Nevine! who as a young woman had advocated the need for a woman to work and her right to love a man of her choosing, or to live without one, if that was what the woman wanted. The questions 'You're wearing a hijab? Since when?' that Mona wanted to suppress burst out of her mouth. She immediately felt the need to offer some explanation, if not an outright apology, for what must have come across as condemnation. But Nevine pre-empted her, good-humouredly admitting, 'Yes, here I am, wearing a hijab like scores and scores of other women,' and hugging each other again, they both tacitly agreed to drop the subject, at least for the time being.

Nevine's hijab made Mona self-conscious of her own hair, slightly plum since her most recent visit to the hairdresser. She would have gladly hidden it under a beret, except that hats, including berets, looked ridiculous on her.

'Let's grab a taxi, go home and drop off your suitcase – you travel very light, I'm impressed. I'm still hopeless when it comes to packing – then let's go out for lunch, just the two of us so we can really talk. You'll get to see the children and Hassan this evening,' Nevine said. 'I keep on referring to them as "the children" but they're men now – two big men. I feel so tiny standing next to them. They even dwarf Hassan, if you can imagine that!'

'I can't wait to see them. They were tiny when you all came to New York, and such great fun,' laughed Mona. 'How long has it been since we last saw each other?'

'Seventeen years.'

'No, it cannot be!'

'Yes, seventeen years!'

'Why so long? Why didn't we make an effort?'

'You tell me!'

'Remember how much we disliked each other when we first met? Who'd have thought at the time we would end up best friends, you and I?' Mona said. 'I could tell from your body language that you took an instant dislike to me. What was it about me that rubbed you the wrong way?'

'I've been meaning to ask you the same question. It was obvious that you weren't keen on me either,' Nevine replied.

'I asked first.'

'You had the reputation of being prodigiously intelligent, so I assumed you were arrogant, perhaps in part because you were reserved. Even aloof,' Nevine said. 'Your turn now.'

'I was jealous. You were so attractive. That's the simple truth,' Mona answered.

'But you too were good looking.'

'Not in the same way,' Mona said.

'What way?'

'A sexy way', Mona said. 'You *know* you were sexy!'

Smiling, Nevine asked, 'Me, sexy? Really? Sexy?' She seemed to enjoy saying that word.

'Yes, sexy,' Mona insisted.

'Well, you were attractive as well as brilliant. You were a genius at maths.'

'A genius? You forget that I flunked my PhD program! And look at you, you're a lawyer,' Mona said.

'And no longer sexy,' Nevine stated in a neutral tone.

'Always sexy, despite the hijab,' Mona quipped, before hurrying to add, 'I'm just teasing.'

'You haven't changed, Mona. Same spirit, same smile, and, I'm sure, as brilliant as ever, even if you didn't finish your PhD. And anyway, you didn't need that degree. You've had one good job after the next.'

'And one husband after the next. I'm as free as a bird. A divorcee again, third time around. I should draw the proper conclusion: marriage is not for me.'

'Marriage is oversold,' Nevine said as she put her hand under Mona's arm, guiding her towards the exit.

The two women, both short and round, walked out of Heathrow Airport arm in arm.

'It's not raining, it's not cold, and it's the end of January,' Mona exclaimed. 'I'm very lucky.'

'You brought us the sun. I don't mind the weather in London. It's not that bad. And it rarely gets hot. I can't stand the heat anymore. Remember how we used to bake in the sun for hours on end at the club and in Alex? We were foolish young girls,' Nevine said.

'You've grown to like living here,' Mona observed.

'It's home now,' Nevine said. 'It's not a matter of liking or disliking. Here's our taxi. We haven't had to wait; what a pleasant surprise! Please, don't strain your back. The driver will handle your suitcase.'

In the taxi, they decided to have lunch at a restaurant on Edgware Road: they both had their heart set on eating *ful medames* and *tamiya* cooked the Egyptian way.

While waiting for their waiter to bring some appetisers, Mona and Nevine looked at each other with affection. For a moment, they were quiet. It was a good, friendly silence which Mona broke by suggesting, 'Let's go to Egypt while the scent of the revolution is still in the air. Who knows how much longer it will last. It feels funny – actually wrong – not to be there right now.'

'What revolution?' Nevine said dismissively.

'Still a sceptic?'

'Increasingly so,' Nevine said. 'How could I not be, with the Muslim Brotherhood and the Salafists controlling Parliament? These people are no believers in democracy.'

'It's curious that you're so down on them.'

'Why? Because I pray five times a day, fast and wear the hijab? Mona, I don't want religion to be shoved down my throat. I don't need the Muslim Brotherhood, or worse, the Salafists to tell me how I should be conducting my life.'

'But religion is not *all* they're about. They talk a lot about social justice.'

'So you, a secular Egyptian, a divorced Copt, are willing to give them the benefit of the doubt! I can hardly believe it.'

'I'm trying to think positively about what has happened. And I'm trying to understand. Despite our regular visits to Egypt, we and the likes of us have been so out of touch with what's really going on in our country. We've been blind. And deaf too! How else would you explain the election results, such a huge number of Egyptians voting for Islamists, Salafists included?'

'I'm not about to consider it a positive thing that so many Egyptians voted for the Islamists.'

'I didn't say it was, but it's better than what we had.'

'What makes you so sure, Mona? What?' There was irritation in Nevine's voice.

'Nevine, the country had reached rock bottom. You know this as well as I do. Just look at what happened to that young woman who was dragged down the square, half-stripped and beaten up; and she's only one of many. Do we want these army men or the security forces to keep doing this?'

'We talk and talk and talk. We talk without really knowing what's happening. What I do know is that if I were to return and live under a regime of self-righteous, two-faced Islamists, I would be tempted to remove my hijab. I really would!'

'Still a revolutionary at heart,' Mona smiled, 'always contesting. You haven't changed at all.' She paused. 'It's far too early for us to tell what the Islamists will do with power in their hands. But we know what our generals are doing. And what they're doing is ugly.'

'I really don't feel I'm in a position to assess the facts, Mona. And many, many questions go through my mind.'

'But Nevine, just think of that terrible episode involving that young woman! Everybody saw what was taking place.'

'Everybody, everybody... who's everybody?'

'Come on, Nevine! Don't tell me that you doubt it ever took place.'

Just then, the waiter appeared with many more appetisers than Mona and Nevine had ordered. 'On the house,' he said. 'In honour of the revolution.'

Knowing that the waiter was a Copt, born and raised in Shubrah, Nevine questioned, in Arabic, 'Are you really celebrating?'

'Change is good,' he said.

'From a distance,' she said and went on, her tone softer, 'But honestly, why would a Copt be celebrating when it seems more and more likely that the Muslim Brotherhood and the Salafists will be controlling the lives of Copts in Egypt? Are you planning to go back?'

With his eyes on Nevine's hijab, the waiter looked surprised. 'At least with them, the Copts will know where they stand, whereas with Mubarak and his people, they were used and abused, while at the same time being told that the government was their only salvation.'

Mona chipped in, 'The Copts themselves can be very intolerant – forgive me for saying so. I myself am a Copt.'

'Yes, however —' the waiter began explaining, but he had to hurry away in response to his boss's signal from the kitchen.

'The Americans are probably helping the Brotherhood and are behind much of what is happening,' Nevine was now asserting.

Tempted as she was not to engage in the discussion, Mona could not help but remark, 'I was under the impression that the Americans were supporting the generals. Mind you, one day the Egyptian newspapers tell us that the Americans are supporting the young revolutionaries; the next, the pro-Mubarak forces and now you tell me they are helping the Islamists. Can they be so undecided?'

'They're trying to keep all of their options open,' Nevine said. 'They've no coherent strategy.'

'We know that they're incompetent. Still, you would expect some minimum consistency on their part. They're going to get burnt no matter what they do, and maybe they deserve it. If you take the long view, they've behaved pretty badly over the years.'

'It must be hard to live in America,' Nevine said. 'I don't know whether I could manage it. You used to complain a lot about it being a tough place.'

'The people are tough, both in good and in unpleasant ways.'

Mona did not have a chance to elaborate, for Nevine interjected, 'The parliamentary elections shouldn't have been held before a constitution is in place. The army made a big mistake by allowing the elections to go ahead. Now the Muslim Brotherhood will want one of their men as president. They'll end up with both the presidency and parliament under their thumb. What a disaster that'll be!'

'The Muslim Brotherhood insist that they won't have a presidential candidate,' Mona said. Talking about Egypt with Nevine was deepening her desire to go there, yet she was beginning to feel that it would be best for her to go without Nevine.

'Mona, I'm scared. I'm really scared, and you should be too!' Nevine suddenly confessed in a loud voice. Then in a quieter voice, as though talking to herself, she continued, 'But perhaps all this was inevitable, perhaps we have got to go through it once and for all so that we can put it behind us. Like a nightmare you must have in order to be freed from it.'

Taken aback by the intensity of Nevine's feelings, Mona did not know how to respond. Before she knew it, though, she was asking her old friend, 'Why the hijab, Nevine?'

'Hassan has asked me that question many times. He still does, every now and then,' Nevine said in response.

Mona decided not to press her, saying instead, 'You and Hassan were our models when we were young and forever thinking of love. You seemed made for each other: free thinkers, free actors, free everything. You, Nevine, were so far ahead of your time – to have gone with him to Paris before you were even engaged, and not to have done it in secret. You two were barely twenty and it was *your* idea!'

Nevine said nothing. She did not even smile.

Mona went on to say, 'Everybody's parents were scandalised as well as terrified that their daughters might do the same. We cheered when you got married a year later. Not only because we were happy for you, but also because it proved our parents to have been dead wrong to assume that you would come to regret that trip. Did I ever tell you that my mother was sure Hassan would leave you? She once said to my father, in my presence, "Why would that boy bother marrying a girl with whom he is clearly having an affair? They didn't go to Paris to hold hands! They could have just strolled along the Corniche". She was obviously trying to send me a message. As if she hadn't already filled my ears with her moralizing. And here you are, still together almost forty years later. Could the secret be that you postponed having children? Whatever you did, it worked.'

Suddenly Nevine looked tired and much older. It shocked Mona to see her so transformed. 'Are things all right... I mean between you and Hassan?' Mona said.

'Oh, things are all right.'

'Really?'

'Yes, if you put aside the affairs we had.'

'You... affairs...' Mona softly said.

'Yes, we both had affairs. Mine was a while ago and Hassan's was more recent. You see, we're no different from most couples,' Nevine stated, not looking at Mona.

'Does Hassan know about the affair you had?'

'Yes, he does, he does.' Now Nevine was speaking fast, 'I was thinking of leaving him; it was more than an affair. I couldn't hide it. I didn't *want* to hide it – I was in love, Mona, madly in love; and love does not care how old you are. It can make you crazy at any age.'

'And how did Hassan take it?'

'He was very upset. Still, he behaved impeccably, as you would expect him to. He told me I had to decide what it was I wanted – that he wouldn't stand in my way.'

'I'm not surprised. That's Hassan, totally Hassan. Was it before or after the two of you and the boys came to New York?'

'After,' Nevine said, looking sideways. 'The boys were still very young, though. It's as if someone else lived this love story. I can't connect the person I have become to the feelings I had then, and to how much I wanted to leave and start all over again.'

'Start what?'

'Life, it seemed to me at the time.'

'You never wrote to me about any of this, not a word! How come?'

'I was too wrapped up in the whole thing. Asking myself every day, several times a day, 'What do I do now?' Feeling ecstatic one minute, then miserable, sometimes both at the same time. Yes, you can feel both happy and miserable. I didn't mean to fall in love. Things had been all right between Hassan and me. Love happened out of the blue and when it was all over, what would have been the point of writing to you about it? I buried it, as deeply as I lived it.'

'How did it end?' Mona asked hesitantly.

'It did Mona, it did… How do these things ever end? Never well.'

'I mean, who ended it? I hope you don't mind my asking.'

'We both did. Nabil – his name was Nabil – didn't want Hassan to get hurt, and I wasn't really prepared to leave Hassan.'

'Nabil? Do I know him?'

'No, no you don't. He lives in Egypt now. The irony is that Hassan thought highly of him, even after I told him what was going on. And Nabil thought highly of Hassan.'

'Was he unattached?'

'As free as can be, divorced and without children. He remarried a couple of years after our affair ended.' She continued a moment later, 'It's strange how I find it difficult to call it an affair, even though that's what it was.' After another pause, Nevine added, 'His wife died not too long after they got married, from cancer, as far as I know. He's on his own now.'

'So you're not in touch with him.'

'No. I'm not in touch.'

'And what about Hassan's affair?'

'It was Hassan's way of getting back at me. I don't mean consciously, but I think that, for a very long time, he was angry with me for having fallen in love with someone else, so he went ahead and decided to do the same.'

Mona thought it best not to question this interpretation. Nevine would not take well to the suggestion that, like her, Hassan might have simply fallen in love. 'How did you react?' she asked.

'With honesty. I was hurt, and I was bitter. I didn't hide it. Look, I had made the choice to stay with him. I had made a big sacrifice. And what did I get in return? Him having an affair and justifying it by telling me that this woman was his "soulmate". Nevin looked Mona in the face, 'You seem surprised, but that's exactly how he put it. "She's my soulmate," he said. I'm not making this up.'

'I find that so difficult to believe,' Mona exclaimed. 'To us all, *you two* were soul mates. What more was he looking for?'

'When I calmed down, it occurred to me that he must have wanted not only his own love story, but also the experience of being with a woman who would make him feel in charge, who would make him feel that he was his own man. He needed that. I had exerted too much influence over him. When we got together we were so young, and though we were the same age, I quickly became his guide, whether we were talking books, movies, politics, relationships between men and women, you name it. I will sound conceited but it's undeniable that, to a large extent, Hassan is who he is because of who *I* am. He told me that himself. I moulded him far more than he moulded me. His affair was also a kind of rebellion against the role I have played in his life.'

This explanation made more sense to Mona than his falling in love as an act of retaliation.

The waiter was finally back with enough *ful medames* and *tamiya* for at least four diners. This time, however, he did not linger at their table; the restaurant had filled up. He smiled apologetically before running to welcome new customers.

'Hassan is no longer with that woman,' Nevine was saying now. 'She was married, and she and her husband moved to Canada. She's Egyptian, half Egyptian, younger than us but not so much younger. No, you don't know her. She grew up in Beirut.'

'Now tell me, why the hijab?' Mona asked.

'It's not what you think,' Nevine began defensively before falling silent. When she resumed speaking, her tone was less tense. 'I didn't look at myself in the mirror one morning and, seeing little beauty left, decide that it was time for a hijab the way an older woman chooses to hide behind big, dark glasses. I don't believe that you ever fully see how much your good looks

have gone, how you're no longer the same person physically. You
see it without seeing it; it doesn't quite sink in. We talk a great
deal about having aged, having put on weight, looking terrible,
but do we really see ourselves as we have become? In any case,
my reflection in the mirror is not the reason I'm wearing a hijab.'
Nevine stopped talking, picked up a slice of pitta bread, played
with it, then put it back in the basket.

'You're keeping me in suspense...' Mona said.

'I'm wearing a hijab because of a vow I made,' Nevine said.

'A vow?'

'You don't believe me, I can tell.'

'I believe you, I do,' Mona replied, doubting now that Nevine
would actually tell her the full story.

To her surprise, Nevine immediately went on to explain,
'While Hassan was in the midst of his affair, he had a cancer
scare – and I had very unpleasant thoughts. I was so confused
and harboured so many negative feelings that I vowed to become
a practicing Muslim – hijab and all – if Hassan came out of it all
right. And he did. But you know, I was always a believer, even
though I never talked about my faith and didn't practice. The
only change is that I have become a *practicing* Muslim. Hassan
doesn't know about my vow. I don't want him to know.'

'You could have become a practicing Muslim without adopting
the hijab,' Mona thought of saying, but she was losing interest
in that subject, just as she was losing interest in hearing Nevine
talk about her life. She was overcome by a wave of exhaustion
which she attributed to jet lag and having eaten almost nonstop
while listening to Nevine, who had only nibbled. Something like
resentfulness was creeping into Mona. As always, when she and

Nevine got together, they rarely talked about her own life. She had never understood why that was the case, whether it was just a pattern which, once established, was not easy to break, or whether it was due to reticence on her part or disinterest on Nevine's. For no obvious reason, today it bothered her that Nevine had never once asked her how she felt about being childless.

'Is the jet lag catching up with you?' Nevine said with concern. 'You look a bit tired.'

'I've been eating too much, and you've eaten nothing,' Mona said, finding it strange that Nevine had put on weight, if she always ate as little as she had over lunch.

'If you'd like me to, I'll go to Egypt with you,' Nevine offered.

Mona briefly closed her eyes and rubbed them.

'Are you all right?' Nevine inquired, her voice anxious.

'Yes. I'm fine,' Mona said. 'A bit of fresh air and sunshine would help, so let's pay our waiter, go for a bit of a walk and then go home. I'll have a nap, if you don't mind.'

'Sure,' Nevine said, after which she once again offered, 'If it will make you happy, let's go to Egypt.'

'Let's talk about it tomorrow. You've almost convinced me that going to Egypt might not be such a good idea,' Mona answered. Trying to sound light-hearted, she continued, 'Is it my turn to cry? Dreams of revolutions… of being part of something that has meaning… of belonging… we can't stop dreaming, can we?'

'I have,' Nevine said. 'Perhaps we can only do so much dreaming. I seem to have exhausted my quota.'

Max

Max lingered in bed, thinking that he had put off
responding to Jack's email for too long. He really
ought to tell him whether he was serious about
going to Egypt with him. Now he could hear the church bells
ringing. He liked their chime, though not quite as much as the
muezzin's call to prayer. In recent weeks, his imagination had
been playing tricks on him and the almost constant hissing and
swishing in his ears reminded him of the muezzin's call, making
those enervating sounds more tolerable.

Summer had not officially started, yet the heat was already
implacable. With the Easter vacationers long since gone, the
only buzz in the village was that of bees, wasps and mosquitoes.
According to the local paper, mosquitoes would be plaguing
the village all year round from now on, for amongst them
was a newcomer; the tiger mosquito, a night and day prowler
that did not know the difference between summer and winter.
'Things aren't what they used to be,' the villagers took to
lamenting in the evenings, as they sat on stone benches that
jutted out from the walls of their maisonettes. 'After us, the
village will die,' one of them would occasionally sigh, half
resigned but also half proud, for it is gratifying to think of
oneself as indispensable.

Guido and Mauro were two pensioners who had spent their entire working lives in Switzerland and had recently returned to the village to enjoy life, they said. Despite their bad hearts and bad knees, nothing seemed to please them more than toiling in their olive groves, vineyards and vegetable gardens. While taking turns helping each other, they discussed politics and talked about their native country the way one would talk about lovable but unruly children. Both believed that Italy was a mess and that most of its politicians should be jailed. Still, they had no wish to end their days anywhere else.

In her mid-fifties, Anna was young by village standards. Physically handicapped from birth, she rarely got out of her chair, made especially for her by her uncle, a master craftsman. Though ninety years old, the man still enjoyed zipping through the village on his *motorino*, often after one too many glasses of wine. The old carpenter was Max's neighbour and kept him well informed about the village's goings-on. 'Anna has suggested to our village priest that having African refugees settle in the village could be a way of breathing new life into it. She thinks that our priest might like that idea, since he is from the Congo,' he had reported to Max, shaking his head in manner that made it clear he did not approve of the idea.

Nearing seventy-five and fluent in Italian, Max was the only foreigner in the village; it had been home for him for just over three years. Apart from his time in Egypt, this was the longest he had resided anywhere since leaving his native California at twenty-five, with an MA in English, 500 dollars in his shirt pocket, and a duffle bag into which he had thrown one pair of jeans, two sweaters, two shirts, two undershirts, three T-shirts, one pair of shoes, four pairs each of socks and shorts, a camera and Dante's *Divine Comedy*.

Nowadays, he considered himself fortunate to have left Egypt before the onset of the revolution. He would have felt uneasy witnessing it as a foreigner while partaking – as he was bound to have done – in the endless ruminations it was giving rise to. Could it have been predicted? Did the young revolutionaries lack the wherewithal to deliver a credible program? Might Baradei be too out of touch to deliver a credible program? Could the Brotherhood be trusted? Would the Salafists ever amount to a significant political force? Were the Copts better or worse off under Mubarak? Would Mubarak and his sons be tried fairly? Would democracy eventually prevail? He would have found it especially hard to listen to expats discuss these questions, as if their primary interest lay in the fate of Egypt when their real concern was, for the most part, 'Will I be able to continue living in that country?' And yet two months ago, when the revolution was still fresh, he had been tempted to go back for a visit, although he could not have explained why. To pay a visit to Martha's grave? He did not much believe in rituals.

Max had no illusions: throughout the whole of his forty-seven years of living in Egypt, he had been a foreigner, which had not been the case for Martha, who had become much less of an outsider as time went on. That is how it had seemed to him, at least. Perhaps the secret had been Martha's aversion to analysing Egypt and her embracing it simply as it was, which was ironic because he had been the one advocating the need to experience rather than intellectualise situations. Or, perhaps the secret had been Martha's not so secretive affair with an Egyptian man, Mahmud H. But even before that affair, she had been in her element in Egypt.

'Would you care to join me on a world tour with no set destinations?' he had asked her, right after getting his MA. 'First we spend a year learning Latin; then we go,' she had stipulated as a condition. Amused and impressed, he had agreed and then, on an impulse, he had suggested they get married, since it would make travel easier. Three weeks later, they were husband and wife and laughing about it after a quick ceremony. She was twenty-five and he was twenty-three. By the end of their year of learning Latin, he had been tempted to propose studying the subject for another year. Mornings spent sleeping in and then making love, followed by studious afternoons during which he and Martha would compete for the attention of a retired Berkeley professor who on some days had seemed besotted with her, and on others, with him. It may have been his technique of getting them to master the Latin declensions. The man was the best sort of eccentric, charging them only a nominal fee for lessons that lasted well beyond the scheduled hour. Their living they had earned at night, he bartending and Martha waiting on tables. None of the blues which newly-weds can succumb to did they experience during the first year of a marriage that lasted forty–six more, till her death at seventy-two. He had been formidably in love with her, their first year. And had been almost in love with himself, judging himself to be handsome when he was plain-looking, profound when he was merely clever. To love oneself when one is in love with someone else is a blessed thing. If only for that reason, that year would be worth re-living a thousand times over, he thought whenever he reminisced, which he did more and more often in the seclusion of his quiet village.

'What's your bet? We come back and live here?' Martha had asked him as they were boarding a plane bound for Amsterdam. 'My hunch is that we won't,' he had replied. 'Mine too,' she had said, nodding her approval. San Francisco was great, but it was not quite enough for him. Back then, 'experiencing the world – not just seeing it' had been his motto. 'One ought to let oneself experience it without predetermining where and how' was what he used to proclaim in fits of youthful bombast. And what had Martha wanted out of their open-ended voyage? He had assumed that he was the principal reason she was undertaking the voyage. Later, much later, she would tell him that she had wanted to see the world, for seeing is experiencing; was her artwork not proof of it? At first, he had not known what to make of her paintings, a mix of stark realism and abstraction, of soft and harsh, light and dark, surprising juxtapositions of scenes and vistas from different countries. He had found it difficult to connect the paintings to the Martha he knew, or thought he knew; and for that reason had been resentful. That Martha had plenty of talent had been immediately clear to him. He had been envious, knowing full well that he lacked any creative ability. Strange how things unfold; her painting, which he had begrudged at first, would gradually cement his attachment to her. Whenever another woman was acquiring an importance in his life that threatened their marriage, whenever he was toying with the idea of being free to do with his life exactly as he pleased, some new painting of Martha's would rekindle his desire to live with her. There was something vibrant and untried in most of her paintings, even as she got to be in her seventies. It was only towards the end of her life that her work became appreciated. Then, suddenly, it began selling like hot cakes. Max believed her relative lack of success all those previous years had been liberating, allowing her to paint with no market in mind.

His first infidelity had been with a girl called Jenny, idling her summer at the Gezirah Sporting Club. The girl had told him she was twenty though she was barely sixteen. Having persuaded herself that she could not live without him, unbeknownst to him she had arranged a lunch meeting with Martha to plead her case. 'I can understand your being in love with him because I am too,' Martha had said to the lovesick teenager who, at a loss for a comeback, had blurted out how old she was. 'She's beautiful but much younger than you think, only sixteen,' Martha informed him in the evening. He had put an end to the affair. The girl would console herself in the arms of a man older than him, someone with whom he used to play the occasional game of squash.

If it had not been for a casual conversation in a café in Istanbul, he would never have ended up working in Egypt. Someone had told someone else, to whom they had happened to talk in that café, that the American University in Cairo was looking for a person who could teach English and creative writing. 'Should I apply?' he had asked Martha. 'Why not?' she had said.

They had travelled to Alexandria by boat, arriving there at dawn on December the twenty-third, 1964. Exhausted from nights of sea sickness, they had decided against going straight to Cairo and instead had a cab driver take them to a hotel – any hotel. The weather had been wretched, with rain pouring down and hail pelting an Alexandria that was nothing like the Alexandria of their imagination. After hours of sleeping, they had tried to see some of the city in the evening, but had only managed to wallow

in water, since it was still raining torrents. They had taken refuge
in a café and heard the loud broadcast of a speech Nasser was
giving in Port Said. Naturally, they had not understood a word
of the speech. Reading it in translation in the English paper the
following morning would give them a succinct introduction to
the current state of American-Egyptian relations. In his speech,
Nasser was inviting the American ambassador to quench his
thirst by drinking water from the Mediterranean if he was
unhappy with Egypt for sending arms to the Congolese rebels
fighting Tschombe. And if the ambassador was still thirsty after
drinking water from the Mediterranean, he could drink some
from the Red Sea too, Nasser had gone on to say. *But will there
still be an American University in Cairo?* had popped into Max's
head while he was reading the speech. 'Should we even bother
going to Cairo?' he had asked Martha. 'I must see the Sphinx,' she
had said. 'Not the Pyramids?' he had exclaimed. 'The Pyramids
too, but the Sphinx first,' she had insisted.

You teach a course for forty years, at the end of which you
conclude that you have wasted your and your students' time. It
happened to Max who, on nearing retirement, had become a
firm believer that creative writing ought to be scrapped from the
syllabus of any respectable institution. All the years he taught
it, he would instruct his students never to begin writing a story
unless they had a solid idea of what it was about. Before putting
pen to paper, they must make up their minds whether it was
about love, lust, friendship, death, betrayal, disillusionment,
cruelty, kindness, tenderness, or what have you. Otherwise, the
story was bound to fall flat. 'But what if it's simply about life?' a
student had asked him one day. He had had to repeat 'Simply

about life?' twice with a slightly derisive intonation to mask his being stumped for an answer. The best he could come up with was a lame 'Life is too grand an idea'. The student had had the last word with her pithy riposte, 'Life, an idea?' He was smitten. They would become friends. If Martha had not fallen in love with her Egyptian writer around that time, who knows what might have happened between him and Nadia, his bold and charming student? Finding it especially galling that Martha's lover was handsome, intelligent, and very likeable, he had not wanted to give her any excuse to leave him. Had Mahmud H been a lesser man, might he have been less determined to preserve his marriage?

Martha had not left Max, but she had not forsaken her lover either – a love that Max was now convinced had been the love of her life. If he were to go back to Cairo, he thought that he would very much like to get in touch with Mahmud H. He knew from mutual friends that, despite his age, the gentleman went every day to Tahrir Square to express his firm support for the revolution. When Martha was alive, in rare moments of generous lucidity, Max had gone so far as to admit to himself – never to her, though – that she would probably be happier living with Mahmud H than with him. Since her death, he had been feeling increasingly guilty for having stood in their way. Unforgivably stupid things he had said to her once, including that having an affair with an Egyptian, even marrying him, would not make an Egyptian out of her; that she should grow up and accept her Americanness; that no matter how wonderful a man Mahmud H was, an unbridgeable cultural gulf separated her from him; that she had taken this whole

Egypt thing far too seriously and far too far. His diatribe came back to him while he lay in bed listening to the church bells. The years had not erased this ugly memory, and Martha was not here to receive his apologies.

It was only later in the morning as he sat down at his computer to email Jack that Max pictured himself going to Cairo, meeting Mahmud H and offering him the apologies he owed Martha. Foolish as this idea seemed, by the time he was starting to compose his email to Jack, it was growing on him. However, he did not commit to his Cairo trip; instead, he wrote that he was feeling too old to be observing a revolution from close quarters, but tomorrow, he might feel younger.

The next day, while reading *Al Ahram* online, he came across a brief mention of the death of Mahmud H from a sudden heart attack in Tahrir Square. 'No better way to die if one's old' went through his mind, just as he heard a knock at the door.

He ignored the knock at first. There was another knock, more pressing this time. Now he could also hear men's voices. He roused himself and went to open the door, wishing he had not moved as he wanted to be alone with his thoughts.

Mauro, Guido and the old carpenter had come to invite him to go to a fiesta in a nearby village. 'I lost a friend,' he told them. They offered their condolences and stayed with him, keeping him company for the rest of the evening. They thought he looked quite shaken. Come the summer there would be many more fiestas to go to, they promised.

As soon as they left, he retreated to his bedroom. The moon was shining through his bedroom window. It was a full moon, he lay down fully clothed and looked up at it. 'As beautiful as the moon' was an expression he had learnt in Egypt. Mahmud H's death and tonight's full moon were making him realise how much more attached to Egypt he was than he had imagined being, or had wanted to be. 'It's my turn now but I have no revolution to live or die for,' he uttered, with some vague longing, and perhaps also a touch of envy.

Hookah Night

S ome were saying that the revolution had ended. Others believed it was still unfolding and, like all revolutions, it was bound to be unpredictable. Of course, there were those who thought the 'real' revolution was just beginning. Then there were the experts calling it a 'coupvolution' to underscore the military's continuing grip on the country, and those who argued that there had never been a revolution, only a rudderless uprising on which the Islamists had shamelessly capitalised.

It had been a year since that thing – call it revolution, 'coupvolution', uprising, Arab Spring, Spring of Arab Discontent – had erupted in Egypt. 'Does it matter what you call it?' the young and loquacious manager of a drab pension in Cairo was asking his lone guest. A few streets down the road, men raging at the suspicious failure of the security forces to keep order in a soccer stadium in Port Said were hurling stones against the concrete and barbed-wire walls surrounding the Ministry of Interior. The guest agreed that it did not matter. What mattered to him was whether it was safe enough to venture into the streets, since he had an appointment. Besides, spending the evening sitting on a wobbly armchair, or lying on a bed with creaky springs in his shabby room in that dilapidated pension, the kind of place that some tourists boast of having discovered, held no appeal to him.

He had booked a room there because it was cheap, expecting it to be as run-down as he had found it. He liked the manager, an affable man who was unsparing in the advice he gave to the guests in English he was rightly proud of.

'You never know what to expect in Cairo these days,' the manager confided. 'I can't believe I'm saying this. Cairo used to be so safe that I'd let my wife walk to the corner store in the middle of the night whenever she got it into her head that she needed something that couldn't wait till the morning. I never worried about her being out. Cairo used to be the safest city in the world. Sure, they could steal your wallet but they would not hurt you. A year ago, I would have told you, "Sir, nothing very bad can happen to you here." I would be lying if I said so to you now. The trouble is that you can't tell the good ones from the bad, you never know what may get you into trouble. We're afraid, and we're afraid to be afraid – so we must pretend that we're not *too* afraid. Do I want Mubarak back? No sir! The revolution was – how do you say it, sir – there must be a revolution. Mubarak wanted his son to become president. The Egyptian people cannot accept this. Mubarak was in his own world – a world up there,' he said pointing towards his head, 'not in the world of the people. Mubarak had to go.' The telephone rang, but before picking it up, he raised his voice to add, 'Many more people must go.'

The guest, Sam, decided to risk going out. He could easily pass for Egyptian. He was not sure whether that was a plus or minus. On the manager's advice, he took his Canadian passport along. Just in case they mistook him for an American, one of those democracy promoters who are really troublemakers and, underneath it all, are believers in America's right to rule the world. No, he did not want to be thought of as one of them although, for the first time in his life, he felt half sympathetic towards America. To try so hard!

'How many foreign journalists had come to Cairo for reasons other than to report on current events?' he asked himself. Probably none other than himself.

He made his appointment. His sense of orientation hardly ever failed him, and after an uneventful walk, he found the café. Each with a hookah by his side, the two men he had arranged to meet – an old Nubian and a Cairene, no longer young but not quite middle-aged either – were waiting for him.

At the café, there was no whiff of the fighting taking place in front of the Ministry of Interior. The customers' loud conversations were punctuated by the bangs of domino and backgammon pieces on the tables, which shook with each clack.

When they first heard Sam speak English, several of the patrons nearby stared at him. Their eyes were not hostile, merely curious. Still, their staring made him uncomfortable. His unease must have communicated itself to the two men he had come to see, as both were parsimonious with their greetings. Nevertheless, they were quick to offer him a hookah. He accepted and sat down.

For the longest time, the three men did not exchange a single word. They merely took steady drags on their hookahs, seemingly oblivious to each other's presence.

So here I am, in a country I can't figure out, in some dirty café facing a dark alley – the sort of café that looks ideal for illicit rendezvous – sharing a table with a scrawny cat that occupies much of the table top and refuses to be chased away. Dizzy as well as sick to my stomach from smoking tobacco that's too sweet, I am about to interview an old man who may not have all his wits about him. All in the hope of getting some revealing information about the death, many years ago, of a Canadian diplomat many Canadians – I would bet most – have never heard of. My translator seems to think that I'm a spy though I made it clear to him that it's not the present that interests me, only an obscure bit of the past. A spy pretending to research the life and death of a diplomat accused of being a spy; not bad material for a novel.

Why is this waiter, who is moving as if he doesn't have a second to spare, serving us tea? I don't recall us ordering any. Is this how things are done in Egypt? You sit at a table and tea gets served, whether you asked for it or not. It's piping hot. There must be some trick to holding the glass without getting scalded; the old man has almost finished his. He has quite a memorable face, with his high cheekbones and deep-set eyes. They're the eyes of a young man, not an old one. Will he let me take his photo?

If he were still alive, my father would be telling me to 'get real'. How he loved that expression, and how I hated it! Only five years before I turn fifty, the age he was when he died. It's been twenty years since he died and I haven't grown any fonder of him. It's frightening how I can't recall ever feeling simple, solid affection for him.

Perhaps my memory isn't so good, pity I have no brother or sister to compare notes with. Might my mother have made me see him in a different light? 'Her heart suddenly stopped working' is all I ever managed to extract from him about her death. Perhaps it was unfair of me to expect him to say more. Perhaps there was nothing more to say about it. It wasn't just her death he wouldn't talk about, though. He would not talk about her, full stop.

I know nothing about his life in Cairo. Did he used to sit in cafés like this café? Did he ever play backgammon? I don't know where he lived, what his father did for a living. 'There is no point in dwelling on the past,' he would say. Another one of his favourite expressions which suited him only marginally better than 'get real' and irritated me just as much.

No profession escaped his criticism. Lawyers were rapacious, engineers obtuse, architects self-important, doctors mechanistic, teachers know-it-alls, journalists fibbers, historians avoiders. And what was he? 'An inventor!' I can still hear him declare – an inventor whose inventions invariably came to nothing. His stories, about why everything he touched failed and why every woman who walked into his life walked out, were all so incredibly contorted. He never tried to make them sound even half plausible. It was as though he relished the opportunity simply to tell them, and didn't care if the picture he gave was that of a life riddled with disappointments and failures. If only his stories had been entertaining, but they were dull. To have a failure for a father is baggage enough, without dullness adding to that weight.

Perhaps it was to irk him that I got both a teacher's certificate and an MA in history, and then applied for a reporter's job I never thought I would land. 'You mustn't like me very much'. If he had said just that and nothing more when I told him that I got the job, there would have been hope for us. For a moment, I thought I could grow to like him. But that was a glimmer of possibility he quickly stamped out with his rambling attack on the media in all its forms. I sometimes think he did not want me to like him. But why? Ironic that I have him to thank for this trip: penniless as he was, he's funding it. He would be cringing at the thought that I used his lottery winnings to come to Egypt and research the death of a Canadian diplomat few have heard of.

'He died instantly,' they told me. 'The driver feels terrible, but there was nothing he could have done to avoid him. Your father crossed the street on a red light, oblivious to the traffic.' They seemed to intimate it was a suicide, which it may have been. They also said, 'He didn't suffer.' But how do they know? How do they know how it feels to die instantly? Did he see the car zooming towards him? Hear the thump that threw him up so high that his body landed metres away? In his pocket – not in his wallet – was the lottery ticket the nurse at the hospital handed me the next day. An unlucky man: hard up all his life, and then he dies with a winning lottery ticket in his pocket, a ticket that ends up in the pocket of an unloving son.

Am I here to irritate him, wherever he now happens to be, by wasting time and money – his money – digging into a forgotten bit of history and visiting a country on which he had turned his back? Because he may have killed himself, as Herbert Norman apparently did? Because Norman's widow made me feel so terribly inept during the first interview I ever conducted, I have felt from that moment on 'I must get this story right'?

It was truly a lamentable performance on my part. What was I thinking, asking her 'And who do you think killed the ambassador, Madam?' five minutes into the interview! My only excuse is that she had done so little to put me at ease or make me feel competent. She looked so cross and daunting that day, nothing like the sweet lady I had been told she was. And then that clumsy question followed by a sneezing fit, and I had no tissue! The appalled look on her face! She might as well have ushered me out of the room.

Really, there's little I can expect this old man to tell me besides what I already know, namely, that a couple of days before Herbert Norman jumped from the roof of a building, Norman had asked him to take him to the rooftop of the embassy and, once up there, had behaved strangely, looking down from the roof in an unsettling way.

I wonder how many diplomats of Norman's era who spent time in Egypt concluded, as he did, that the Islamists should be more of a concern than the communists. He was prescient. Well, I doubt that I will actually write that biography; it's a project I shelved for too long. Now it feels too much like an assignment, not like something I want to do.

I could, instead, write a piece on the life of a Nubian in Egypt, from Faruq's times till the present. That old man might be willing to help me. I must remember that his name is Adel. I know nothing about Nubians so it would be an opportunity to learn something. Herbert Norman would consider it more worthy a subject than his life and death.

My translator will ask himself why I've changed my plans and will become suspicious... I wonder how he will react, whether he'll continue to work for me.

He's a strange one, handsome but with big circles under his eyes; he looks like he hasn't slept well in ages. I don't like seeing men look so tired. Dr Herbert – may he rest in peace – looked exhausted the week before his death. Tonight though, I don't care to talk about what happened to Dr Herbert. I'm sad enough about the state of affairs in the country.

I bet there's some Egyptian blood in that man, even though he asked no questions about Egypt last time we met. Only questions about Dr Herbert. He doesn't seem interested in Egypt at all, unlike those Egyptians and their children who spent most of their lives outside the country and have come back to dip one foot in while keeping the other one abroad. Many of them must be asking themselves whether they should be going back to where they came from. Few of them will stay once the Muslim Brotherhood is firmly in control. I have nothing against the Brothers. I'm not for them either. I'll withhold judgment, wait and see how they run the country. Can they run it though? They definitely want power. Those who think that they'll be easy to dislodge if they mishandle affairs are deluding themselves. Things can't get much worse anyway. If they don't make a total mess of it, they'll be in power for years to come. And if they're a big failure, who's to say that the Salafists will not be next in control? It's a far-fetched possibility; still, despair could drive people into the arms of the Salafists. All this talk about the Muslim Brotherhood and the Salafists devouring each other and self-destructing in the process may be wishful thinking.

Now the Salafists, I have no time for, none whatsoever. I'd hate to see them in power. We know all too well how those who back and fund them behave as soon as they leave their country and come to Egypt to breathe some fresh air: pure in their country, impure in ours. My grandsons think that I worked too long with Westerners, that it colours my views. It's funny because they're the ones who talk nonstop about democracy, whereas I never do.

I don't care about democracy. What I want for my children and grandchildren is meat on the table – not even every day, twice or three times a week would be enough – it could be lamb, beef or veal. And I want some fairness, not heaps of money at the top, nothing at the bottom, and very little in between. A pyramid upside down is how money is distributed in this country. We want the pyramid the right side up! And fairness would mean that the same rules apply to the big, rich thieves as are applied to the small, poor ones. From what one hears about Western countries, including America, democracy doesn't guarantee this.

Our big thieves have been very active in Nubia, selling some of our most valuable land to the Saudis. It's time something was done about that. The Nubians deserve justice too in this 'new' Egypt the young people are so euphoric about. We Nubians should be careful though. We're Nubian, but we're also Egyptian. We don't want the rest of the country to forget that.

There was a time when I longed to go back to Nubia and die there. I was young then. Now that I'm old, it doesn't matter to me where I die. Here, there… it's God's will anyway.

So this man – Sam, he calls himself, which makes me wonder whether his full name is Samir – has flown all the way from Canada to investigate the death of Dr Herbert. But he's not even a relative of his and the country is a shambles. It makes no sense. My children told me to be careful, he could be a spy, but why would a spy bother interviewing me about Dr Herbert?

He seems to think that the Americans killed Dr Herbert. Sure, they did. The Americans have a very long hand. They're behind everything, but that doesn't mean they always get what they want. They usually get what they don't want. Dr Herbert was probably saying things they didn't like. That's why they went after him.

He wasn't a spy. You can tell if a man is honest. I could tell that he was an honest man: he understood Nasser, the good as well as the bad side. He was wise. 'A ruler with too much power cannot remain good, even if he's a good man at the outset,' he told me, and he was right. All rulers with too much power end up ruthless. Perhaps we do need a bit of democracy.

'We need a Nasser now,' the translator was telling me earlier.

The man wasn't even born when Nasser died. All he knows is from hearsay and rumours. Yes, Nasser was relatively honest; he didn't steal. Or if he did, he didn't steal much; he didn't fill his family's pockets.

In those days, nobody stole much. Nobody had a lot of money. At first, I liked Nasser. Who didn't? Men wanted to be Nasser, and all the women longed to marry a Nasser. Like everyone else in the country, we Nubians were impressed at first and we loved him too for a while. But, unfortunately, he didn't give us the same in return. We ended up paying a tall price for his High Dam. We got a pittance for losing our lands when we had been promised a paradise. What we got was a crumbling paradise where the houses they gave us kept collapsing. It wasn't just because of what happened to us that I changed my mind about Nasser though. His using informers and having neighbours spy on neighbours, employees on bosses, even officers on their superiors, poisoned the air of the whole country. Today, who remembers that in the early sixties he jailed four French diplomats and a couple of their Egyptian employees? His allegation that they were spying was just a trump card to free Ben Bella whom the French had put in prison.

At least that was a worthwhile cause. It isn't obvious what our generals are up to, threatening to jail this group of Americans, along with a few Germans and their Egyptian employees. It's a dangerous game for Egypt, and not only because the Americans might retaliate. There is another danger lurking there. The Saudis might offer their services as mediators. Slowly, slowly, they might end up running the country. The generals think they can handle them and remain on top of the situation, but can they? The power of money! Thank God the Saudis don't like to part with it so they cannot put too much pressure on us. Qatar is another story – its ruler will pay to get what he wants. But what does he want? Not democracy, it's the last thing on his mind. He's no democrat in his country.

We should be holding those people accountable for interfering in our affairs. And to think that Nasser was so concerned about the Arab world that he got us involved in Yemen's wars. And tried to unite us with Syria! Arab countries, rich or poor, have never done anything but give us trouble.

I would love to know how much this translator is getting paid. My English wasn't bad, but that was a long time ago. I have forgotten most of it, lack of use after I stopped working. I should have suggested my grandsons do the translating, their English is very good. They could do with a bit of money.

This Canadian, he really is a strange man. He comes, sits down and hardly says anything. I don't think he's a spy. If he were, he'd be talking more. I must tell him that he looks Egyptian. He might open up a bit.

The old man is a bit muddled, and my instinct tells me that the Canadian has a hidden agenda. I was tempted to report him to the

*police as soon as he approached me; something about him made
me nervous. But it's difficult to turn down money these days, and
the money he's offering isn't bad. I hope I can understand him
well enough. I'm good at guessing. Still, I find him hard to follow.
I've no problems with the English, though the Americans and
the Australians are very difficult to understand. The Americans
mumble even when they speak loudly, and the Australians
whisper. I thought the Canadians were more like the English. Not
this one! The real reason he's in Egypt will become clearer tonight.
I don't mind foreigners coming to Egypt, even living amongst us,
as long as they respect our customs. Egyptians like people, but we
don't like them poking their nose in our affairs. If he takes a taxi
to return to his pension and I have any suspicion, I could have a
word with the taxi driver and suggest a stop at a nearby police
station.*

*I don't want to rush to conclusions. We'll see what happens
when he interviews the old man. I'm not seeking trouble for
trouble's sake. I'm tired of all the chaos, and of people talking about
the revolution. When will it all be over and done with? We need a
firm, guiding hand.*

*My mother's a good judge of people. She still gets teary-eyed
whenever Nasser's name is mentioned. He made mistakes, but
who doesn't? As for what happened in 1967, it was Amer's fault.
That's a fact. If that pleasure-seeking addict hadn't overseen the
army, things might have gone differently for the country. We can't
blame Nasser for leaving Amer in charge of the army. He tried to
side-line him, but Amer had the army's support, support that he
had bought, showering his men with perks, everybody knows that.
Nasser's detractors claim that he had Amer killed after the defeat,*

but he had no need to get rid of him that way. He could have put him on trial for gross incompetence. There's no question it was a suicide; Nasser was a man of integrity.

This old man believes that the millions who flooded the streets to ask Nasser to stay on – my father being one of them – were paid to demonstrate. I don't want to argue with him, it's inappropriate to argue with an old man. Respect for the elderly is something that's quickly disappearing in this country. Mubarak was no good and enriched himself at our expense. However, putting him on trial is not right and proper. We should send him abroad and take his money, as was done with King Faruq. What will likely happen though is that we'll put him in a pretend jail for a while at least, and he'll get to keep his money. We'll never get the money, the real money. His sons, on the other hand, are another matter. They should be tried and taste life in jail. Gamal Mubarak isn't even smart. If he were smart, he wouldn't have tried to take his father's place now. He would have waited for a few years before running for office. He would have had a much better chance then. The fools advising him, who must have got tons of money for their lousy advice, should be tried too. They say that it was his mother who wanted him to succeed his father. A man who lets his mother tell him what to do is a child, not a man, let alone a leader. They also say that she's been paying thugs to loot and burn and wreck the country. I bet that Israel and America are behind much of the mayhem. It's in their interests for Egypt to fall apart. And Canada too is right behind Israel. We can no longer assume that Canada is fair. Americans, Canadians, they're all the same, bowing to Israel and wanting the Arabs weak. It makes my blood boil.

***

The three men were having their hookahs refilled. Waltzing between the tables with a tray balanced on the palm of one hand, a waiter was shouting advice to the board players on their next move. Sam still felt dizzy but the nausea had passed. He was beginning to enjoy his evening. Egypt was starting to feel less foreign.

Looking at the old man as though talking to him directly, he said, 'I'd like to ask Mr Adel a few questions about Nubia, if that's all right with him.'

The old man answered with two nods. The translator smiled knowingly before saying to Sam, 'Of course.'

Dawn was breaking and an acrid smell of plastic burning was in the air when Sam came out of the military police station. A shiver ran over him; his eyes twitched and stung. He could make out a few grey buildings in the distance and leading to them, this treeless, carless road. He had no idea where in Cairo he was.

Behind him, his taxi driver and the translator were arguing loudly.

Question after question he had had to answer, all night long. Why was he interested in Nubia? Did he think that Nubians were being ill-treated? How about the Copts? What organisation was he working for? Surely he was being paid for his research: by whom? What was his organisation's ultimate objective? What did he think of Egypt's revolution?

Two officers fluent in English had interrogated him. After stripping him of his cell phone, camera and tape-recorder, they had left him waiting for a couple of hours before beginning to grill him. They had been reasonably polite throughout, although every now and then they would hint at how lucky he was to be dealing with them rather than some of the other officers who could be infinitely tougher. When they had discovered that his father was Egyptian, their tone had hardened somewhat.

'Why did your father leave his country?' the stouter of the two officers had asked him several times, refusing to believe that Sam had no idea why, and that his father had avoided talking to him about Egypt. 'No Egyptian who leaves stops talking about his country,' the officer had insisted.

'Egypt never leaves you,' the other officer, who was tall and quite dashing-looking, had added. Hearing Sam explain that he had come to Egypt to do research on a Canadian diplomat driven to suicide by the Americans, that same officer had remarked that agent provocateurs often wave the anti-American flag.

Through more questions, they had found out that Sam had grown up motherless, and both had offered him their sympathy. The heavy-set officer had then asked, 'Do you know that you're Egyptian since your father was Egyptian? You're Canadian only on paper.'

Sam had winced. For no reason he could have articulated, the statement had rubbed him the wrong way.

'You seem upset. Why? You don't want to be Egyptian?' the handsome officer had inquired. 'Don't worry; we won't keep you in Egypt against your will. If you were younger, we might; you might have had to join our army and fight our wars.' The two officers burst out laughing.

In the pause that followed, he was offered lukewarm, overly sweet tea, pitta bread and slices of Greek cheese. Then the questions had veered towards Canada, the nice-looking officer claiming he was interested in emigrating there and going so far as to suggest that he might contact Sam in the future, to get a better idea of what Canada had to offer. If foreign elements continued to play havoc with Egypt, people like him might be driven to leave it, even though they loved it, the officer had said, looking straight into Sam's eyes. Wondering whether the officer was setting a trap for him to fall into, Sam had refrained from responding.

The interrogation had ended with them telling him that he was free to go, though without his tape-recorder, cell phone and camera. While shaking his hand and holding it longer than Sam thought necessary, the powerfully built officer had stated in a manner that managed somehow to seem both friendly and threatening, 'We're not as bad as foreign papers say we are. Write this about us. And stop worrying about the Nubians. The Nubians are our business. If you want it to be your business, you should come and live here. It is your country after all. We won't keep you out of it.'

Sam could now hear the taxi driver yelling. He knew enough Arabic to guess that the driver was asking the translator 'You're happy now?' and demanding compensation for his night's lost fares.

Sam reached into his pocket to get his wallet out, only to remember that it too had been confiscated. The driver, who just then happened to be looking in Sam's direction, gathered that Sam wanted to give him money but could not find his wallet. Feeling sheepish about the night's events, the driver offered to drive Sam back to his pension for nothing. 'We people. You and I people. Brothers,' he said to Sam in English. Then, raising his face as well as his arms towards the sky, he invoked God's blessings on all.

Against the pension manager's advice – there was more fighting around the Ministry of the Interior – Sam went back to the café that evening. He was hoping to find the old man there again. He was not disappointed.

I Have Made Up My Mind

June 1, 2012

Gamal called me shortly after midnight. His voice was hoarse. I had been fast asleep when the phone rang. He called me 'sweetie', but I didn't feel sweet at all. Then he said that he had made up his mind – he would vote rather than abstain; he would vote for Shafiq. Almost in the same breath, he announced to me that he was going to initiate divorce proceedings. 'Why now?' I asked. He didn't like the question. What was he thinking? Was I meant to say 'hurrah!' and jump on a plane to London?

'I don't understand you. What is it you want, Ann?' he said. 'To go back to sleep,' I answered, which was a mean thing to say, so I apologised. He apologised too, for having woken me up. We sounded nothing like lovers anxious to fall into each other's arms.

I asked him what made him decide to vote for Shafiq. He said that, in spite of his military background and his close connection to the Mubarak regime, Shafiq was the lesser of two evils. There wouldn't be even a semblance of democracy with Morsi as president.

He hasn't given up trying to convince me that the day I decide to stop teaching, Egypt will lose its appeal for me. Last night, we joked about my being the outsider who wants to be a part of Egypt, and him being the insider who is happy to be out of it. It's funny, but not so funny, that my thirty years of living and working here don't seem to count for much – I'm still viewed as an outsider by him and Egyptians in general. And yet I don't want to leave. That's the paradox.

Today is the twentieth anniversary of mother's death. I nearly forgot about it. I seldom think of her now. 'The nomad', her friends called her. 'Experiences' and 'discoveries' are words I came to dislike, hearing her use them to justify pulling up stakes, over and over again, with me in tow. Crossing countries and continents seemed to be child's play to her. There was a reckless quality about everything she did – quite an admirable quality, really. I owe her Egypt, so I should be grateful; I *am* grateful. If it were not for her passing infatuation with it, I wouldn't have come for a visit and decided to stay. She of course moved on, to Turkey for a little while, then Yemen... I would need a whole page to make a list of her short-lived passions.

The revolution is reviving old friendships. I have been hearing from friends who live abroad, and with whom I had lost touch. They want to know what's happening. As if I know. As if *anybody* living here knows. Does Tantawi[1] even know? Tomorrow, we should find out what fate awaits Mubarak. The court is expected to render its decision. Like everybody else in the country, I talk or think politics all day long. The irony is that I was never interested in politics before. Like mother, who despite

1 Mubarak's long-serving minister of defense and de facto head of state from the ousting of Mubarak on February 11, 2011, to the inauguration of Mohamad Morsi on June 30, 2012.

her interest in the world, never listened to the news or bought a newspaper.

I don't know whether to believe that Gamal will divorce Maggie; he didn't say that he has told her. I didn't want to ask him if he had.

'It's not so simple, Gamal,' I emailed him after we had hung up. Girl meets boy. They fall in love. They get engaged. They quarrel. He criticises her for being a hopeless flirt. They break up. She finds comfort in someone else's arms. He ends up in those of a close friend of hers. But then the girl gets gravely sick and he pays her a visit. They reconcile and quickly marry; she refuses to have anything more to do with the close friend. A couple of years pass and then he meets the friend by chance. He tells her, 'We should talk.' They end up having an enduring affair, despite their best efforts at breaking it off.

Will Maggie ever talk to me again? As I get older, it bothers me, more and more, to think that she might not.

June 2, 2012

Gamal called early in the morning. After an upsetting conversation in which we both accused the other of thoughtlessness, we agreed not to contact each other for a while. Until after the elections, I suggested. I was being flippant, but he took me seriously and said that, by then, I might be clearer about what it is I want in life, since I would no longer be as absorbed by events in Egypt. He must be thinking, 'She is fifty-five, was never married and here I am offering her something solid, but she's having second thoughts. It makes no sense!'

Am I supposed to feel bad about being preoccupied by what's happening in Egypt? The verdict in the Mubarak trial was predictable: a life sentence for the killings but not guilty on the corruption charges. If they had absolved him of wrongdoing for the killings, they would have been faced with more protests. And if they had found him guilty of corruption, it would have opened a can of worms.

Demonstrators in Tahrir Square are very upset about the verdict and are calling for a new revolution. What surprises me is that the military have not gently done away with Mubarak. It would have been an easy thing to do, since he is apparently gravely ill.

I had to put up with another annoying visit from my landlady. Why did I ever bother renting a place in Maadi for the summer when I could have stayed in my own apartment downtown? The idea of having a taste of life in a relatively quieter, greener part of the city wasn't such a brilliant idea after all. Fawzeya always uses some vague pretext to land on me at very short notice when all she wants is to make sure I haven't pinched or broken any of her precious possessions. Today, she went on and on about her cousin, the King, insisting that, if he had not been deposed by 'a gang of thieves', Egypt would virtually be a Switzerland. Incensed by the verdict in the Mubarak case, she's hoping for a *coup d'etat* by leaders strong enough to rid the country of those she calls 'hooligans masquerading as revolutionaries'. Isn't there a bit of a contradiction there? She laments that 'thieves' deposed her cousin, yet she supports Mubarak, a product of their regime? Before leaving, she criticised America for encouraging the 'hooligans' and not standing by Mubarak. 'Your government will come to regret it,' was her parting shot.

I'm tempted to call Gamal and ask him to be patient – not an unreasonable request. I was patient all those years. Since he introduced the subject of divorce, I think of Maggie a great deal. In an ideal world, the three of us would sit together and sort it out.

June 3, 2012

It's increasingly hot, so hot that the riot policemen standing around the court house were eating ice cream when the verdict was rendered.

More protests in the country over the Mubarak verdict. People are chanting: 'Salafists, Secularists, Copts and Brothers are one!'

Abla came this morning. I wasn't sure she would. What a gem! She cleans the house without any fuss, has interesting things to say but knows how to leave me alone, too. She asked me how Gamal is doing. I'm sure she suspects he's married. Though glad that Mubarak is gone, she surprised me by saying that she is also a touch sad because the Mubarak years were a big part of her life, and this part has now ended.

The phone rang early this morning. I was hoping it would be Gamal so I rushed to pick it up and almost tripped on a rug. It was Fawzeya who wanted to let me know that, if I wished to stay for another couple of months after the end of the summer, she would have to increase the rent by thirty percent for additional months. She kept harping on about how expensive life has become before warning me that foreigners, particularly Americans, are being watched, so she is taking a risk by renting her place to me. Does she think I'm a fool? Were she reasonable, she would try to entice me to stay by offering to lower the rent. Nowadays, foreigners are leaving – not seeking – apartments. I let her know that I have no intention of renewing the contract, as I'm planning to return to my apartment. Her tone immediately became icy. I cannot wait to leave.

No word from Gamal. I haven't called or emailed him either. How things change. Years ago, we couldn't have resisted communicating with each other, no matter what. I cannot imagine life without him, but I cannot imagine everyday life with him either.

Could Maggie be the one initiating the divorce? He didn't sound himself when he called to tell me about it.

June 13, 2012

At home with a bad case of lumbago for over a week now. At thirty, one thinks, 'Damn this lumbago.' At fifty-five, one thinks, 'I'm old and getting older.'

It has got me down. Nelly told Gamal about it and he called right away. We're back to talking every day, but our conversations are not free-flowing, like they once were. No mention of the divorce and little mention of politics as he finds it a depressing subject, so we run out of things to say.

Hoda came and brought a pile of books for me to read. She's very nervous about the elections and what may happen to the Copts, should Morsi win. She would love to go to Canada. Her husband and children refuse, however; they say that Egypt is their country too.

June 14, 2012

Confusion reigns. The constitutional court declared part of the law under which Parliament was elected invalid, so Tantawi quickly dissolved Parliament. The Islamists are upset, of course. The court also decreed that Shafiq can run. Out of this quagmire, will Tantawi eventually come out the winner? Some think that the Brotherhood will get the better of him and, while they may not mind sharing power with the military, they'll want their own man to head it.

Gamal didn't call this morning. If I were in Maggie's shoes, I would have left him long ago. He has never told me that he doesn't love her.

June 15, 2012

The wait begins, the elections are tomorrow and the day after. Everybody in the country is on edge and constantly listening to the news or reading the papers, looking for clues about what's happening behind closed doors. Most people I have been talking to, including Gamal, think that Shafiq will win. I think that Morsi will.

When I was out on the balcony this afternoon, I heard the *bawab* next door yelling at his wife and son that they should vote for Shafiq and not Morsi – what the Brotherhood wants is money and more money. 'They'll get rich and will give thousands of reasons as to why it's not a sin,' he shouted.

Abla was evasive when I asked her who would get her vote. I take that to mean that she'll vote for Morsi; I suspect she believes that a foreigner would want her to vote for Shafiq.

My back has much improved. And Gamal called. He was very loving. He said that he'll be coming at the end of the month, that there's much we need to discuss. When I heard his voice this morning, I realised how much I have been missing him. I can't wait to see him. My unease about the divorce – a subject we continue to avoid – reflects in part the guilt I feel towards Maggie. *Should* I be feeling guilty? She and Gamal had broken up before he and I got together; I'm not the reason he left her. She, however, is the reason he left me. A case of shared guilt? I doubt that she has come to see it that way.

June 17, 2012

Both Morsi and Shafiq are claiming victory and accusing each other of cheating. We should know the results within the next three or four days. Rumours are already circulating that Tantawi and his men will tamper with the results to ensure Shafiq's victory.

Egyptians are making fewer jokes these days. People are tired. It has been sixteen months since the revolution and it's not clear where the country's going.

Gamal didn't call. I tried to reach him but he was out of the office all day long.

June 18, 2012

Even though the results are not out, the Brotherhood has already announced that Morsi has won. The Supreme Council of the Armed Forces responded by restricting presidential powers, which gave rise to a huge demonstration in the Midan.

Abla is clearly excited about Morsi having perhaps won. As I thought, she did vote for him. She was incredulous when I said that if I could have voted, I would have done the same. Gamal got very annoyed when I told him that last night. He said I needed to get out of Egypt to gain some perspective. I saw little point in arguing with him over the phone.

June 19, 2012

Still no results! Mubarak is on life support at a military hospital near Cairo. So they claim.

June 20, 2012

Still nothing! What is being cooked up behind closed doors? I have spent the last two days doing nothing but waiting for the results to be announced.

My back finally feels normal again, just in time for Gamal's arrival. He confirmed that he's coming. I'm excited! We haven't seen each other in almost two months. I wonder how he would take it if I were to ask to meet his father. I've been wanting to meet his father for a long time, but I have never summoned the courage to suggest it. I think I will when he comes.

June 22, 2012

Nothing yet, except for a claim by the army that it will use force against anyone threatening the interests of the country. Does this mean that Tantawi is about to declare Shafiq the winner?

Intelligence is no bar to tactlessness. Hala, who is unquestionably very sharp, phoned me from Montreal and said that her Egyptian friends in Cairo are too affected by the events for her to be bothering them with her phone calls. She obviously views me as an outsider who is not much affected. It upset me that she sees me in that light. I should have told her how she made me feel.

June 23, 2012

They promised to give us the results tomorrow. My physiotherapist, with whom I had a good session this morning, did not vote. She thinks that the revolution is dead. She implied that I'm a naive foreigner for still believing.

June 24, 2012

It's Morsi by a narrow margin. Egypt's first non-military president since 1952. The Brotherhood is celebrating in the Midan. I'm not sure how I feel. Numb, I think. Gamal must not be pleased.

Another shouting match between the next door *bawab* and his wife. I heard him scream that she would be weeping soon, since Morsi would show his true colours before long. His son kept pleading with him to stop being so pessimistic. But he didn't manage to silence his father, who pronounced it a day of mourning.

A good joke worth remembering – asked why he did not run for president, Tantawi said he didn't want to give up power. Will Morsi bring the military under control? Recent polls suggest that the Egyptian people want the military to relinquish power to a civilian government.

John – whom I hadn't heard from in ages – called and sounded ecstatic. He believes in the wonders of Islamic financing. My telling him that I am as thick as a brick when it comes to economics did not stop him from trying to explain to me why he thinks Islamic financing can cure Egypt's problems. Next month is the fiftieth anniversary of his arrival in Egypt. He has been teaching for all those years! It strikes me as far too long.

I really want to talk to Gamal; I called countless times but couldn't reach him. Has he sunk into a big funk over the election results? I doubt it. He's worked hard at detaching himself emotionally from Egypt and seems to have succeeded.

I'm exhausted, but yes, I am hopeful, even if I have some trepidation. The Islamists in power may prove to be all right. That so many people are surprised by their victory is what surprises me.

Maggie used to be fairly political. I wonder what her thoughts are today, whether she and Gamal see eye to eye on what has been happening in Egypt.

June 25, 2012

The celebrations continue. 'Down with military rule!' is the overriding sentiment being expressed across the city. I ought to throw a little party. I have been too much of a hermit this month; it's time to live normally again.

Gamal and I talked at great length. He's convinced that Morsi will be at the Brotherhood's beck and call, that some officers must be sympathetic to the Brotherhood and that Tantawi may not last now that Morsi is president. We also talked about the children, how they might react to a divorce. He seems confident that they'll take it reasonably well. I disagree. But we'll talk more when he comes. I have yet to ask him whether he has broached the subject of divorce with Maggie.

June 26, 2012

It should not matter, but it does to me, that Maggie thinks I had designs on Gamal when they were engaged and she and I were close friends. Would she believe me if I told her that this wasn't the case? That I fell in love with Gamal well after they had broken up, listening to him talk to me about his father – this father both she and I had assumed to be dead? Was it the tale itself, the way Gamal told it, or his confiding in me the existence of his father that touched something in me so irrevocably? I can still see myself, see Gamal, the Lido, and even the waiter who got him his beer; I can see the whole scene in minute detail down to what we were both wearing that day. I wonder what *he* remembers of that accidental meeting, whether he remembers it as well as I do.

> *I am at the Lido, reading. I hear a familiar voice say, 'Can I join you?' It's Gamal. He looks out of sorts. I would rather continue reading, but I invite him to sit down, expecting that he'll want to talk about Maggie. I have mixed feelings about him. He's a bit too sure of himself for my liking. I don't dislike him, but I don't particularly like him either.*
>
> *He orders a beer. I'm still drinking my guava juice. He asks me what I am reading but pays no attention to what I say. Twice, I have to repeat 'Buddenbrooks'.*
>
> *I'm looking for some excuse to get up and leave, so that I can finish reading my novel somewhere else in the club, when the waiter returns with beer and peanuts. While pouring himself a glass of beer, Gamal informs me that he has just come back from seeing his father. Before I can say anything,*

he begins to recount, in a flat tone – very unlike his usual ebullient tone – how his father had been drawn to politics from a very young age; first to communism, then to socialism, then to the Muslim Brotherhood; that he had also written poetry which his own father had never bothered to read, although his mother had been supportive and thought he had talent; that at the age of twenty he began having alternate bouts of euphoria and depression. A couple of years later, his moods were more even, and to his parents' surprise, he agreed to an arranged marriage and to work at a bank. However, the emotional ups and downs returned; he started drinking, stopped writing poetry and resigned from his job; he would disappear for long stretches of time – once he went missing for a whole week – without telling his wife or parents his whereabouts. The day before Black Saturday, Gamal's mother entrusted her one-year-old son to her husband's parents and left, never to return. The morning after Black Saturday, Gamal's father had some kind of fit during which he claimed to have been one of the arsonists responsible for setting Cairo on fire, so his parents had him admitted to a mental institution, where he has remained since. 'My grandfather pretended my father was dead. I always sensed it was not true, but I found it convenient to believe him,' Gamal acknowledges. He also tells me that he learned all this from his grandmother, but only after the death of his grandfather; he was fifteen at the time – old enough to know, the grandmother said, before making him promise to visit his father regularly.

Gamal continues confiding, 'I just came back from seeing him. Sometimes, he seems quite normal, and we can have a reasonable conversation; other times, he talks nonsense. Today started out well but, at the end of the visit, he said, "You're like a son to me."' With none of his usual self-assurance, Gamal now lets out, 'I don't know if I can keep doing this,' and then, 'You're the only person to whom I have talked about my father.'

Love flowing out of one conversation. Lives radically altered because of that one conversation. That's what happened. Am I deluding myself?

Gamal still hasn't told Maggie or the children about his father. Whenever I suggest that he should, he replies that there's no hurry, that he's not quite ready yet.

June 28, 2012

Last night as I lay in bed, tossing and turning, it occurred to me that I might have been the wife and Maggie the mistress, and that those roles might have suited us better. Perhaps we have actually played them without realising it. Sex could be what kept her and Gamal together, a thought that no longer pains me as much as it used to.

He's on the road and expects to be arriving in Cairo the day Morsi is taking the oath.

June 30, 2012

Morsi took the oath in front of the constitutional court. He had said that he would not, because its judges were appointed by Mubarak, yet he did. Yesterday, as a symbolic gesture, he also took the oath in the Midan. In his speeches – he has given three of them – he promised democracy and real freedom.

It's late at night. I'm worried about Gamal. He should have been here by now. The roads to and from the airport aren't safe, according to Abla.

July 1, 2012

A new dawn? Where do I start? It is five o'clock in the morning, and Gamal is sleeping. We had an argument soon after he walked in. An argument about Morsi which degenerated when he said I should stop trying to be Egyptian, that there are some things about the country I will never understand. I countered that he was being unfair, that he was mostly mad at me for having correctly predicted the outcome of the election. A bit later, after we had calmed down, and while we were having a beer, he asked me whether I cared to meet his father.

Maggie knows about his father. Just before he left, he told her the whole story. I'm no longer the only one to know. It feels odd. Even odder is the fact that I'm experiencing this as a betrayal.

I didn't have to raise the subject of the divorce: he introduced it himself by saying that I was right, it's not so simple.

Ten years from now, where will I be? What will Egypt be like?

I hear the bulbuls chirping. I'll miss hearing them when I return downtown.

Soad

Soad enjoyed leafing through books, though she did not know how to read. Sometimes, she stopped in front of the library's travel section and picked up a book to look at the pictures. Except for two short trips to Alexandria, she had never left Cairo. Her job, which consisted of keeping the library clean and tidy, had been a godsend. It was not strenuous, and the hours were reasonable.

It was the end of the work week. She was setting down books in the tray reserved for reshelving without wiping their covers, which was unusual for her.

Her absent-mindedness did not escape the notice of Sayed, sitting at the reception desk. While he knew that Soad did not fast because of her age and poor health, he thought that she must have been woken up at the crack of dawn by the sounds of family members snacking before their day of fasting, so Ramadan was taking its toll on her too.

He surmised that the heat would not be helping. The building had been without electricity for over an hour; it was already stifling in the library. Out in the street, the temperature had reached thirty-nine degrees and was still climbing.

Besides, President Morsi's unexpected sacking of the army chief must also be preoccupying Soad. It was certainly preoccupying him. Morsi's bold move could set off fresh demonstrations by those seeing it as the beginning of a new dictatorship and the end of the revolution; more instability could result in the library being closed and their jobs evaporating. A half-hearted supporter of Morsi, Sayed was becoming increasingly concerned about losing his job.

In his usual spot and engrossed in his book, the library's sole patron today was an elderly man who dropped in regularly. He often took his shoes off and, as if his toes were in need of fresh air, he would wriggle them out of big holes in his socks.

'Maybe he's cut the holes for that purpose,' Soad had whispered to Sayed, the first time she saw the man's exposed toes. Then she complained that the smell coming from his corner was no laughing matter. This morning the gentleman had kept his shoes on, though sweat was dripping from his brow onto the open book in his hands. Had she been paying any attention, Soad would probably have asked him, in her polite manner, to treat the book with more care, for books deserved respect. However, she never once looked in his direction.

Now in the kitchen, she was quietly making her tea. She sat down and sighed as she waited for the water to boil. She was a firm believer in premonitions. Since last night, her intuition told her that she would soon be 'retired', just like General Tantawi had been 'retired'.

First thing that morning, as they were both stepping into the elevator, Sett Amina had told her to drop by her office at two o'clock. 'That's it,' Soad had immediately thought, her heart sinking. Why would the library supervisor want to see her, other than to tell her that her services were no longer needed?

The water was boiling. Soad poured it into a glass and dropped in a chamomile tea bag, hoping that it would soothe her nerves. Perhaps her hands would be steadier; they were trembling noticeably more than they had for a while.

At two o'clock sharp, she knocked at the door of Sett Amina's office.

Sett Amina welcomed Soad with too big a smile, inviting her to make herself comfortable in the leather armchair reserved for special guests. She then offered to make her a cup of tea, as she knew that Soad did not fast. Soad declined the offer and chose to sit on a wooden chair from which it would be easier for her to get up.

Soad looked down as Sett Amina spoke, for what seemed like forever, about how it was time for her to look after her health and take it easy, to rest and enjoy life and her grandchildren; she deserved to retire, her children would look after her, they owed it to her, she had been such a good mother, they no doubt felt hugely indebted to her, retirement would be fulfilling in its own way, she would quickly come to wonder why she had not retired earlier. Such a long speech, to tell her that her employment was being terminated – for her own good; she truly was a model employee that the library was lucky to have had.

Soad slipped her hands from under the sleeves of her *galabeya* and rested them on her lap. There was no longer any point in trying to hide her hands as she had for months now, whether by covering them with the sleeves of her *galabaya*, by sitting on them, or by crossing her arms and putting her hands under her armpits. Her hands had let her down. If it were not for their tremor, she would not have been made to leave; she had been doing as good a job as ever. She had never missed a day's work. Her performance could not be the issue. It was simply that people were uneasy seeing her hard at work with those unsteady hands. People did not like feeling sorry for her, so they had chosen to fire her.

She desperately wanted to argue her case, argue against this unjustified and unwanted retirement which would give her no pension, only a pitiably small severance package. She wanted to explain to Sett Amina that her work had been her greatest source of satisfaction in life, even if it was work held in low regard, and that she had no desire to depend on her children, dutiful as they might be. Would Sett Amina care to depend on hers? But she knew that protesting would serve no purpose. Besides, she did not want to beg. She was too proud, even to ask if working part-time might be possible. She held her head high as she got up to leave Sett Amina's office.

'Do stay in touch and come and see us often; we'll miss you very much,' Sett Amina said as Soad left.

Back in the library, Soad went straight to the kitchen to gather her belongings. She did not have to take them home immediately since she could keep working for another month and a half, until the end of September; Sett Amina had given her that choice. However, she had already made up her mind to quit at the end of August. The longer she stayed, the harder it would be to go. Leaving at the end of September, when life typically returned to the library, would be especially sad. Best to avoid that!

She shoved a pair of old slippers and a couple of spare *galabeyas* into a large plastic bag, but her nature quickly reasserted itself; she took them out and folded them before placing them back in the bag. She then went to the washroom, where she removed her hijab before splashing her face with cold water over and over again. She repositioned the hijab on her thinning grey hair and, returning to the kitchen, she dabbed onto her nape some of the 555 cologne she kept at work. Just enough cologne to last her for another couple of weeks; no need to pack that bottle. She rested on the chair and looked at her hands. The tremor seemed worse. Now her chin began quivering, which, in her case, was often a prelude to tears. She managed to hold them back. She would have plenty of time for tears at home. Her bag in hand, she took a side exit out of the library. She wanted to see nobody, talk to nobody.

The electricity was back on. As always, Soad took the elevator to avoid the eight flights of stairs to the street. Midway down, the elevator stopped. Was the electricity off again? And if so, how long would this breakdown last? Soad yelled for the *bawab* to come and help. No sign of him. She yelled some more, but still no sign of him. Then, the elevator began moving again, only to come to a jerky stop seconds later, this time, fortunately, at a floor rather than in between floors.

She succeeded in pushing open the elevator door then slowly climbed down the remaining four flights of stairs. Her back was sore. Just as she got to the ground floor, she saw the *bawab* step into the building.

Normally mild-mannered, she shouted, 'Where have you been?' He said that he had been praying. 'But it's not prayer time,' she shot back. He retorted that it was an extra prayer.

In front of the building, a bearded young man she frequently saw asked her why she looked upset. She confided that she had lost her job. He said to her, 'But grandmother, you should be glad. You'll have more time to spend with your grandchildren.'

'And will my grandchildren feed me?' she replied. He laughed, which infuriated her.

'That will teach me for blurting out that I lost my job,' she muttered to herself as she tottered down the street.

Now her chest was hurting; never before had she had that sensation of burning and constriction around her heart. It was already four o'clock, yet the sun was still dizzyingly hot. She looked at the passing cars to see whether a taxi might stop and drive her to the metro station. She did not hold out much hope of that; now was the time when everyone, taxi drivers included, would be rushing home to eat.

The cars kept zooming by. She stared at the coffee shop across the street. She had never sat in a coffee shop in Cairo, only in Alexandria, the two times she had gone there on holiday with her husband. They were very young then. She had thought on those trips that they would love each other forever. How wrong she had been! He was now living with his second wife, two flights of stairs down from her.

On the spur of the moment, she decided to go to the coffee shop, order a mango juice and sit at a table. Thanks to a miraculous break in the traffic, she managed to cross the street.

She collapsed on the doorstep of the coffee shop.

As she regained consciousness, she saw, kneeling by her side, the bearded young man with whom she had had that upsetting exchange earlier. He propped her up and put in her hand a glass of water, which an anxious waiter had sweetened with heaps of sugar. Her hand shook too much for her to hold the glass, so he held it for her, encouraging her to have at least one sip of water.

So many men have a beard these days, my sons too, even the one who hated life in Saudi Arabia, she thought. To please the young man, she had one sip of water before she lost consciousness again.

She woke up in the hospital after what felt like days of dreamless sleeping. Though there was a great deal of noise and talking in the room, she recognised her oldest son's voice. 'Revolutions are made by those who think of today, not by those who think of tomorrow,' he was asserting.

Since when did he become so smart? she wondered. *He never had much to say under Mubarak.* All of a sudden, she remembered that her working life was over.

'Why wake up?' she cried out. Her son rushed to her side.

Without knowing quite why, she pretended that she did not recognise him. 'Who are you?' she asked, listlessly. Shrieking 'My mother doesn't know me,' her son shrieked as he ran to get help.

When he returned with a nurse, she felt ashamed and said by way of an excuse, 'I'm tired, I'm so very tired. It must be that revolution.'

Revolutionary Death

The very evening his favourite grandson was buried – the grandson he had been sharing a room with since his wife's death – Hag Adel had taken to bed, vowing that, for the remaining time he had left in this senseless world, his bed was where he would be spending his days as well as his nights. Only for his ablutions would he get up. Not even to pray. God was benevolent, God would understand, God would forgive him.

Never a big eater, he was now living on small rations of yoghurt and bread. Tea he drank all day long, so much of it that his concerned daughter Safeya had decided to make it weaker and weaker, for which he chided her, though to no effect. 'The day you start eating properly and moving around, I'll let it steep as long as you want,' she would tell him when he grumbled. He pretended not to hear.

'The café is not the same without you. Let's go and smoke a hookah, let's make a hookah night out of it!' his old friends suggested whenever they dropped by to see him in the evening, but he refused to join them. He took to responding to questions monosyllabically, limiting his answers to a 'yes' or a 'no', unaccompanied by a 'thank you' or any of the other niceties about which he had been punctilious in the past. He seemed to have lost his ability to be polite, or perhaps his interest in being polite.

When alone in his room, he often cursed out loud. He cursed Morsi. He cursed the Americans for having any truck with the man and Mubarak for having been so shameful a ruler. He cursed Sadat for having courted the Islamists, the Gulf countries for funding them and Israel for behaving in ways bound to ensure their continued popularity. He even cursed Nasser for having steered the country in the wrong direction and himself, for having once believed that Egypt needed a Nasser.

Whenever she overheard him in the midst of one of his imprecations, limping into his room as fast as her polio-stricken leg permitted, Safeya would urge him to calm down and be reasonable. He would stop cursing but would turn away from her towards the wall and close his eyes.

'It is time for you to pack up and go, ya Morsi,' his grandson, Hossam, had been chanting in front of the presidential palace when he was killed by Brotherhood supporters. By the time he was ten, Hossam was praying five times a day and fasting during the month of Ramadan. He had never touched a drop of liquor. They had murdered the most pious of his grandsons, bludgeoning him with broken bottles and iron rods and calling him as well as the others demonstrating with him traitors to the country, not real Egyptians, unbelievers, beholden to Israel and the West. That was what a survivor of the beatings would report later, the little bit of his cheeks showing from under his beard bruised black and blue, and one of his eyes shut tight. If not for his face being so swollen, the injured demonstrator had told Hag Adel, he would have shaved off his beard forthwith, lest he be mistaken for one of those animals.

With the help of his wife – mercifully spared this grief by her death five years earlier – and unmarried Safeya, Hag Adel had raised Hossam, whose father had vanished a year after his birth. Hossam's mother – and the youngest of Hag Adel's six children – had died in a bus collision shortly thereafter. Family, friends and neighbours agreed that she must have been so shaken and distracted by her husband's inexplicable desertion that she had not been watching the traffic.

'I will look after the boy,' Hag Adel had informed the boy's uncles and aunts who were offering to do the same; and that was what he had done, more attentively than he had looked after his own children. Hossam's first step had filled him with such ridiculous pride that he had invited friends, neighbours, and even vague café acquaintances for a feast of a meal. 'But all children take a first step,' his wife had tried to object.

Now the boy was dead. And the country was being kicked around like a football and rolling downhill fast. Would any good ever come out of that revolution, about which Hag Adel had been guardedly optimistic at first? He had had his worries all along, amongst them the fear that the extremists amongst the Islamists would end up in the saddle. Or, that the ones appearing to be more sensible would decide to use religion as a weapon to silence their opponents.

'No one will be able to muzzle us from now on,' Hossam had tried to reassure his grandfather.

'They'll tell you you're a Nubian, not an Egyptian,' Hag Adel had warned him. 'Forget about politics. You're lucky to be working. Don't do anything foolish.'

'Work?' Hossam had exclaimed dismissively. With his bachelor's degree in commerce, he had hoped to be more than a messenger boy in a bank, a job he had obtained through his grandfather's connections.

What should he, Hag Adel, have done to keep his grandson at home on the ill-fated day Hossam marched to his death? Threaten him? Plead with him? Feign illness is what he should have done. That idea now rarely left Hag Adel, who gradually convinced himself that he could have saved his grandson had he played sick – the boy had been loving and caring and would have stayed at home to be with him.

In the room they had shared, Hossam's bed was made as if readied for the young man's return. The evening of his grandson's funeral, Hag Adel had asked Safeya to remake the boy's bed with freshly laundered sheets.

'This won't bring him back,' she had remarked tearfully. Known never to have laid a hand on any of his children and to be especially protective of her, he slapped her hard. Not once but twice. It was from that evening onwards that he took refuge in his bedroom, ordering Safeya time and time again to turn down the volume of the TV in the adjoining room. He did not want to know what was happening in the country – especially not from Al Jazeera, which was nothing but a mouthpiece for the Brotherhood. 'I wish I was deaf!' he would shout whenever he heard the TV.

Some days later, hearing on the news channel that the parents of two men killed by Morsi's supporters in front of the presidential palace were launching a lawsuit against Morsi, Safeya rushed into his room to pass on this information.

Hag Adel received the news by wailing, 'Leave me alone,' his lips and chin trembling uncontrollably as he repeated his plea.

'Father, it was God's will. Hossam is better off where he is than we are here,' Safeya tried to console him as she rubbed his arm and shoulder. Then, offering to bring him a glass of tea, as strong as he liked it, she hobbled out of the room.

The evening that the results of the referendum on Morsi's constitution were broadcast, Hag Adel insisted that Safeya close his bedroom door.

He had argued with his grandson, 'Believe you me, Morsi is here to stay. Do you really think that demonstrating against him will make any difference whatsoever?' It had made a difference. The other bed in his room was unoccupied now.

The constitution was ratified. Morsi was addressing the nation, his voice penetrating Hag Adel's room. 'Where are you, *ya* Safeya? Turn down that TV,' Hag Adel shouted. '*Ya* Safeya, *ya* Safeya,' he kept calling, but with no success. She must have gone to the neighbours.

That voice, those words! Hag Adel could take it no longer. He would have to get up to mute the TV. His legs weak, his head spinning, unable to walk straight, he slowly crossed his bedroom, stopping to sit for a couple of minutes on Hossam's bed until his dizziness abated. By the time he reached the TV in the room next door, Morsi was declaring that arguments – even fierce disagreement – about the constitution proved the health of the country's fresh and hard-won democracy, and that opponents of the constitution had a right to their opinions. 'Yes, in their graves,' Hag Adel roared. He kicked at the TV but it withstood his swipe, Morsi's voice blaring on. Weeping, 'Murderers, murderers!' Hag Adel sank to the floor.

Safeya, who had heard him howling from next door, came back as fast as she could. 'Father, father,' she wailed in turn while slapping her face, 'none of this will bring Hossam back. Let's give Morsi a chance.'

'Shut up!' he shouted, as he waved away her attempts to get him to his feet. 'Shut up.' Then he surprised her by talking, really talking, for the first time in days, saying, 'For years, those in charge of this country worked hard to prevent ordinary people from making decisions about matters concerning them. Now, those in charge want people to make decisions about matters they know nothing about. And they call that democracy.'

He allowed her to help him get up, and then he staggered back to his room, ignoring her entreaties to continue to the neighbours' and have his first proper meal in days.

'*Ya* Hossam, why aren't you talking to me?' Safeya heard him ask feverishly in the middle of the night. 'Why do you keep disappearing? One minute you're here, the next, you're gone, then you reappear. That's not like you; you don't even say goodbye. What's the matter with you? *Ya* Hossam, sit down for a little while. Sit down, I say! You keep moving; you're tiring me out; you're giving me a headache.' Then he fell silent.

When she shuffled into his room and turned on the lamp, his eyes were those of a frightened child. He asked her, 'Where's the boy hiding?'

She rearranged the covers on his bed and said that he must have had a bad dream; she would make him a hot cup of milk, as the night was cold.

'Yes, milk. Some for the boy too.' As she walked out of the room, he insisted, 'Don't forget milk for the boy.'

If her father was still delirious in the morning, she would call her oldest brother, Safeya decided.

When she returned with the milk, he greeted her with the oddest statement, 'The ambassador never drank the cup of tea I made for him on that *khamaseen* day. I tried my best that day. I tried.'

He drank the milk to the last sip and then began to hum, eyes closed and head gently tilting from side to side in time, 'Oh Golden Nubia what has become of you?' and 'From where, from where that dark-skinned girl whose smile is like alabaster?'

Safeya made up her mind to spend the night in her father's bedroom, but she did not dare sleep on what had been Hossam's bed. Instead, she put a mat on the floor and lay down.

Much to her relief, nothing Hag Adel said the next morning suggested that his mind was still cloudy. Safeya noticed though that he kept yawning, which seemed unusual.

To avoid upsetting him, she turned off the TV, even though it was hard for her to go about her household chores without its comforting sound in the background. Tomorrow her brothers and sister and their families were coming for an evening meal. Might the smell of appetizing dishes persuade her father to abandon his self-imposed seclusion?

'Still sleepy?' she asked on seeing him yawn.

'My jaw aches,' he said, yawning once more, his cheeks as hollow as spoons. He had been thin to begin with, but if they saw him now, Safeya would bet that the children in the alley would call him 'Tutankhamun' behind his back. The possibility that his days were numbered – a thought she had refused to consider until now – thrust itself upon her and, for an interminable moment, she was unable to banish it or the unavoidable question, 'What's to become of me once he's gone?'

It was a question that was not a question. She knew that she would be expected to live with one of her brothers or her sister, whether she went to live with them or one of them moved with their family into the apartment she shared with her father. This would confirm her state as both husbandless and crippled and, so in theory, in need of being looked after, when in fact she would be doing much of the looking after. Many of the household jobs were bound to fall on her shoulders. The work she did not fear – work had never been an issue for her. No, the prospect she dreaded was to find herself under her siblings' thumbs, subjected to the rhythm of their lives, accountable to them.

With her father dead but Hossam alive, she could have stayed in the apartment. Though her brothers and sister would have objected at the outset, they would likely have come round and accepted that it made sense for her to go on living with Hossam in the apartment, since he at least was bound to get married and have a family. Things would have been so different if Hossam had lived.

'The devil take you, you who killed my nephew and are now killing my father too,' Safeya said under her breath.

For the rest of the day she outdid herself, preparing one dish after the next for the family meal. No curses or mumbles came from her father's room. At lunch, she was delighted to see him eat a bit more yoghurt than his customary one bowl.

Trying to suppress their giggles and lower their excited voices – Hag Adel's plight was common knowledge in the neighbourhood – the flock of children that had followed Sam into the building, up the staircase and onto the landing, was making enough noise to bring Safeya to the door even before Sam knocked.

Her immediate thought was that this Egyptian-looking foreigner must be the Canadian her father and Hossam had been talking about, the man who had said he wanted to study the Nubians but seemed to have abandoned that project. Her father had described to her how, after offering him and Hossam a generous amount for their help, the Canadian had not even carried on with the interviews, though he continued to meet them at the café – typically in the late evening, when he would sit with them without saying much for long stretches of time, seemingly content. At the end of those meetings, he would unfailingly give Hag Adel an envelope containing the promised fee, despite Hag Adel's objections that payment was not necessary since they had done no work. Insisting that Hag Adel take the envelope, the Canadian would apparently say, 'Ma'alesh, ma'alesh.'

'I don't understand this man. But I like him. Don't ask me why. I do, I just do. And it's not for the money,' Hag Adel had said to Safeya more than once.

Hossam had been non-committal, saying that it was difficult to form an opinion about someone as reserved as this Canadian who had told them, though, that his name was Samir, that his father was Egyptian and that his mother had died when he was a toddler. 'Like me,' Hossam had remarked. 'But he didn't have a Hag Adel for a grandfather,' he had fondly added.

Although news of Hossam's death had reached Sam a few weeks earlier at the café, it had taken him until now to decide to pay this condolence visit. Though willing to give him the Hag's address, the café regulars had cautioned him not to talk too much about Hossam to Hag Adel, whose state of mind they described as 'fragile'. One waiter had insinuated that Hag Adel was losing his mind, the shock had been so great. Another waiter had observed that, because they themselves are nearing death, some old people become quite detached and hardly mourn the loss of their loved ones. All those who knew Hag Adel well had protested that he did not fall into that category. He was deeply affected by Hossam's death.

While she stood on the landing in front of Sam, all Safeya could think of was that she was wearing the drabbest of her housedresses – the one she reserved for days of heavy chores – and it was not black and it might even be stained. She crossed her arms to try and hide any obvious marks that might be there.

As for Sam, he was wondering whether he should have brought fruits or flowers instead of the box of sweets he was carrying. Never having paid a condolence visit in his life, he was rehearsing in his head what to say to Hag Adel.

In shrill voices, the children explained that men at the café had given the foreigner Hag Adel's address.

Neither father nor Hossam told us that this Canadian was so handsome went through Safeya's mind, before she turned her attention to the increasingly boisterous children. 'Enough,' she ordered them. 'Enough!' Then she uncrossed her arms and stood aside to let Sam in, saying, 'Welcome, welcome, please come in.'

He seemed to hesitate. The children burst out laughing.

Safeya yelled at them to be quiet, whereupon the youngest one, apparently the ringleader, pointed out to her that *she* was being loud. Safeya shooed the children away with a brusque '*Yalla, yalla*, it's time for you to go home.' They ran down the stairs, hollering that they were only trying to help. Safeya promised to give them some treats, but not right now.

When Sam stepped into the apartment, she was so flustered that she neglected to offer him a seat. Instead she went straight to her father's room and left Sam standing in the hallway, his box of sweets still in his hands. Was her father sleeping, or merely pretending to be asleep? Safeya touched his shoulders. He opened his eyes.

'Father, the Canadian is here to see you, with a very big box of sweets. Should I bring him to your room? It would be rude not to,' she whispered.

'What Canadian?' Hag Adel asked.

'But we know only one Canadian, Father. The man interested in the Nubians,' Safeya breathed into his ear.

'*That* Canadian!' Hag Adel said.

What other Canadian could it be? Safeya wanted to ask, but thought it best not to put her father on the spot. 'So, shall I let him in?' she asked softly, even though she knew she would not take no for an answer. She cast her eyes around the room. It was spotless. She had cleaned it that morning. She had even re-made Hossam's bed. Hag Adel shrugged.

'So, is that a yes or a no?' she persisted.

He shrugged again.

'I know that you would like to see him,' she said, patting his shoulder. 'I'll go and fetch him.'

'You always do what you want anyway,' Hag Adel griped.

'But you want to see him, don't you?'

'All right, all right,' her father conceded.

'I'm so sorry,' Safeya told Sam, still standing by the entrance door. As if he were perfectly fluent in Arabic, she went on to apologise, 'Forgive me for not having offered you a seat. But I'm not myself since they killed our Hossam, may God bless his pure soul my father. He's not himself either. I worry about him. He'll be very happy to see you, even if he doesn't show it. Please, come in and make yourself at home.'

With her high cheekbones, this woman reminded Sam of Hag Adel. Her face was regal, her features perfectly symmetrical, her skin smooth and firm, the skin of a much younger woman. He gathered from his conversations at the café that this was Hossam's unmarried, limping aunt whose name now escaped him.

Sam handed her the box of sweets. 'I am Sam,' he said. 'Samir,' as he lowered his eyes, worried that she might think him rude if he continued to look at her face.

She smiled. 'A thousand thanks. It is very kind of you to be thinking of my father, he's waiting for you.' Then she added, as she turned to lead him into Hag Adel's room, 'My name is Safeya.'

Sam adjusted his pace to hers.

Hag Adel was lying on his side facing the wall, his back to the door.

'Your friend is here,' Safeya announced and then gestured for Sam to sit on the room's lone chair.

Hag Adel did not acknowledge them.

'Father, your friend has come to see you. It wasn't easy for him to find us. He probably had to do a big circle around town to get here because of the demonstrations. You know what that's like. He must be really fond of you,' she said and stroked her father's back.

Hag Adel kept quiet.

'I'm going to make some tea, so I'll leave you with your guest,' Safeya told him, still stroking her father's back. 'I'll come back with some of the sweets he brought you. You must taste them. They look so good.'

'Don't come back with tea that tastes like water,' Hag Adel instructed her.

'Don't worry, I won't,' she said, pleased to have gotten a response out of him.

When Safeya turned round towards him, Sam was standing next to the chair. She urged him to sit down. He nodded and quietly brought the chair close to Hag Adel's bed.

Safeya limped across the room.

A childhood memory came back to Sam: memory of the wheelchair-bound girl with violet eyes he had been in love with at age ten, a love he had not dared declare to the girl or admit to his best friend. Whatever had happened to that girl who, besides her arresting eyes, had an insolent nose that made her seem to be mocking the whole world, including him? Had she succeeded in making a life for herself? And whatever had happened to his first real girlfriend? He had never been good at staying in touch with his ex-lovers. It was not as though he bore them any grudges, or that he had lost all interest in them and their lives. He could not explain why he had never made efforts to stay in touch; that was simply how it was. Was he a sentimental or an unsentimental man? Neither... or both?

Sam thought he heard Hag Adel whimper '*Ya* Hossam'. He stood up and, leaning over Hag Adel, he said, in his halting Arabic, 'Hag Adel, I am sad. I am very sad about Hossam. He was a very good boy.'

'*Ya* Hossam!' Hag Adel called, louder this time.

Sam wanted to pat Hag Adel's back, but the thought that Safeya might return any time now held him back.

'*Ya* Hossam,' Hag Adel called again.

Anxiously awaiting Safeya's reappearance, Sam let his eyes wander around the room, from the wicker chair on which he had been sitting to a bulky armoire that took up much of a wall, and then to a small mirror hanging beside it. When his eyes fell on Hossam's metal bed, he immediately looked away as though he had no right to be looking at it.

'*Ya* Hossam,' Hag Adel kept calling at shorter and shorter intervals.

Sam began stroking Hag Adel's back. He had been in Egypt for months but had done no work whatsoever, neither on Herbert Norman, nor on the Nubians. His life seemed to have come to a standstill. No love, no work, no projects. A life consisting mostly of aloneness, of himself. He had no desire to return to Canada despite feeling out of place in Egypt. In this room, however, he felt at home, maybe because he had inexplicably grown attached to this old man.

Safeya's steps in the corridor broke his chain of thoughts. Hag Adel must have heard them too, for he turned over. His eyes met Sam's. He sighed then said, 'Hossam will not join us.'

Nodding, Sam patted his hand. He was alarmed by how much weight Hag Adel had lost, how sunken his eyes and cheeks were.

Pointing at the wicker chair, Hag Adel told him to sit down.

Safeya, who had changed into a black, velvety gown, came in carrying a large tray on which she had laid tea and sweets. 'Your friend is spoiling you,' she smiled to her father. 'He brought you the sweetest of sweets.' Then, speaking to Sam, she thanked him again and pronounced the sweets to be the best in town, made by the finest pastry maker of Cairo.

Sam found himself inordinately pleased at Safeya's praise.

Hag Adel gulped the glass of tea Safeya put in his hand after helping him sit up. He also had a sliver of the tiniest cake on the tray.

'He's afraid to put on weight,' Safeya joked.

The tea was too hot for Sam to drink so he let it sit.

'All this time in Egypt and he still can't drink hot tea,' Hag Adel said, shaking his head.

Safeya laughed softly and said that she would let the two men talk, she had a few things to do in the kitchen but would be back before long.

'You stay, you stay with me,' Hag Adel told Sam. As soon as Safeya was gone, looking out the window he offered, 'If you're tired, you can lie down on that other bed.'

'The chair is good,' Sam said. 'But thank you very much'.

'I may fall asleep, but don't leave,' Hag Adel said.

'I won't,' Sam assured him.

'You drink your tea now,' Hag Adel ordered him.

'I will,' Sam replied and began sipping his tea.

'It can't be good. It's not hot enough,' Hag Adel said, before lying on his pillow and closing his eyes.

Time passed. Sam could not tell how long Safeya had been gone as he had no watch. He had not replaced his when it had stopped working weeks ago. Hag Adel seemed to be sleeping.

Sam sank into a kind of reverie, imagining what it would be like for him to look after Hag Adel, to be by his side as his life drew to a close. An idea that had never occurred to Sam before presented itself to him. It was a simple idea, the kind of idea that makes one wonder *why didn't I think of this before?* It was that, *for a life to be whole, for a life to make sense, one ought to have helped a man meet his end.*

Hag Adel suddenly began hiccupping. 'Hag Adel,' Sam said gently, just as he heard Safeya's limp. He got up as she stepped into the room. Together, they stood by Hag Adel's bed, waiting for him to stop hiccupping. When he did, they sat down, Sam on the wicker chair and Safeya on Hossam's bed, but only after she had insisted on serving Sam another glass of tea. They kept their eyes on Hag Adel and, except for Safeya every now and then in a hushed voice imploring God to protect her father, they said nothing.

Sam began thinking that he could spend days in this room, with this silence. Safeya, meanwhile, was thinking about Canada. She would have liked to ask this Canadian – who was really Egyptian, even if he barely spoke Arabic – if it was true that in Canada, disabled people could lead regular lives, that stores and even buses made special provisions for them.

When Sam eventually thought about leaving, it was pitch dark. He remained seated, however, and must have dozed, since he did not hear Safeya go out of the room and return with a tray on which she had laid a variety of tempting warm dishes.

Hag Adel was wide awake and dipping a slice of bread into a bowl of lentil soup.

'See what you've accomplished,' Safeya told Sam, her eyes sparkling, her smile luminous.

'Eat,' Hag Adel urged Sam. 'Safeya knows how to cook. Her mother was a better cook, but she's good too.'

'How can I not be a good cook when she taught me all I know?' Safeya exclaimed, as she served Sam a bowl of soup.

'To think that I voted for Morsi,' Hag Adel said, and then he stopped eating.

'You voted for Morsi?' Safeya cried out.

Ignoring her, Hag Adel continued, 'Hossam too voted for that man, but he was smart, he quickly figured him out and saw him for the dangerous man he is.'

'Father, your soup will get cold. Eat a bit!'

'You must go back to your country,' Hag Adel told Sam. 'This isn't a place for a man like you.'

Sam chuckled as he replied, 'Not everything's good in Canada.'

Since her father himself had introduced the subject of politics, Safeya felt free to say that a group of Nubians was planning to protest Egypt's treatment of Nubians.

Hag Adel put down the slice of bread he was holding and, pressing on his temples with the palm of his hands, intoned, 'Oh Golden Nubia, what has become of you, why did I ever leave you; Oh Golden Nubia, will you forgive me for trying to forget you; Oh Golden Nubia, we all make mistakes but why should the young and virtuous pay for them...'

If only I could spend the night here, Sam wished.

God's Will

Both his sons were balding and plump. *Why is it I never noticed how much they've aged?* Hag Adel asked himself as he sat up on his bed. He then wondered, *Might they look younger if there was more life in them? They are so wooden.*

The two men stood facing him, their eyes wandering towards the door.

'They should leave since they cannot hide their desire to be gone,' he grumbled, loud enough for them to hear.

His sons cast each other a sidelong glance.

Safeya lingered, going through the pretence of tidying up her father's room.

Avoiding his father's gaze, Amr, the older of the two brothers, finally said, 'This isn't an old man's game.'

'Nonsense! If ever there *was* an old man's game, this is it. Old men have nothing to lose. You're afraid. Shame on you!'

'We're not afraid,' Hussein, his younger son, protested. 'We just don't know if it's the right thing to do.'

'So you want the man responsible for your nephew's death back in power?'

'Father, thugs killed Hossam – God bless his soul – but we shouldn't jump to the conclusion that those thugs were Morsi's men,' Amr said in a tired voice.

'His men or not his men, they are of the same ilk,' Hag Adel declared. 'I don't want the country to be in Morsi's hands for another three years. I shouldn't care as I won't be around for much longer, but I *do* care.'

'Oh Father, don't say you won't be around!' Safeya remonstrated. 'God obviously wants you with us, otherwise he would have taken you last year, when you seemed to have lost all your strength and gave me such a fright. But he has decreed that you're needed here.'

'I would much rather he had taken me – but since he didn't, I will do what must be done. I will go to the Midan and show my support for those who brought Morsi down. I *will* go, whether or not you'll come along,' Hag Adel said, staring angrily at his sons.

Amr tried again, 'Father, you're wrong to assume that we're afraid. The truth is that we don't know what's best for the country. If you don't mind my saying so, anybody who thinks he knows is deluding himself. When Mubarak was toppled, we all rejoiced. Was it such a wonderful thing? We voted for Morsi and celebrated when the results were announced. Were we wrong? Were we right? We want democracy, but we also want the army to be strong and to protect us, we want religion and freedom and tourists. We want to head north and south, turn right and left, all at the same time...'

Hussein interrupted, saying 'We want money, we need money, the country needs money. All the revolutions in the world will not bring us money. We've learnt that.'

'Revolutions bring us the illusion of being alive, nothing more,' added his brother.

'Spare me your philosophising. My grandson knew right from wrong. Are you for Morsi? *Are* you? Speak up! Or go! You keep looking at the door; I'm not keeping you in the room. You are free men. Mark my words though: if Morsi is reinstated, the only free men in this country will be the Brothers. That's the lesson I learnt.'

'Father, you're getting too excited,' Safeya interjected. Sitting on the edge of her father's bed, she straightened the sheets.

'We're being responsible sons. We both think that it would be unwise to take you to the Midan for that demonstration. Things could get ugly. What if we have to run?' Amr clasped his hands behind his back, trying to keep his growing impatience at bay.

'Run?' Hag Adel laughed. Well, you can carry me. I'm as light as a feather.' Looking away from them, he added, 'I'll find some way to go. I don't need you.'

Safeya turned towards her brothers to say, 'He's serious. He'll get there.'

'How?' Hussein said.

The old man declared, 'I'll ask my Canadian friend to take me. I'll go with him.'

'With the Canadian?' both his two sons cried. Then Amr asked, 'What is this Canadian's story, anyway? Does he have nothing better to do than hang around in this chaotic country?'

'There's nothing wrong with a man wanting to spend time in his father's country,' Hag Adel retorted.

'Are you sure his father *was* Egyptian?' Hussein probed.

'Don't meddle in my affairs. He's my friend. I have a solid head on my shoulders, even if my legs are giving way.'

'It's a terrible idea for you to go with him,' Amr argued. 'He's a foreigner, no matter who his father was. Going to the Midan with a foreigner is an invitation for trouble. It's not as if he's a journalist covering events, or a TV man. He's a nobody and therefore an easy target,' Amr asserted.

'And you say *I* am unreasonable! Need I remind you that the men who killed Hossam did not differentiate between foreigners and Egyptians?'

'Foreigners are more vulnerable,' Amr insisted. 'It would be folly to go to the Midan with a foreigner.'

'The folly would be to stay at home when the army is asking us to show our support,' Hag Adel said.

'Haven't we had enough of the army? We had them in charge for years and what did it bring us? You tell us!' Hussein challenged him.

'So you *are* for Morsi after all! Do you really believe that because we elected him we must live with whatever evil he dispenses?'

'Father, even Hossam wouldn't be happy with the army playing the role it's playing. You yourself were not keen on the army ruling the country,' Hussein continued.

'Don't you tell me what Hossam would have or would not have approved of,' Hag Adel cried. 'I raised that boy. As for my change of mind, well, circumstances have changed. I would be a fool not to change my mind. That's what minds are for!'

'Some say that Sisi is very devout, that he and the Brotherhood are not so far apart,' Amr observed.

'Then why did he decide to support those opposing Morsi?' Safeya asked. 'I don't understand anything anymore. In the past, things were not good, but at least they were clear. Now it's become all so confused. Thinking makes me even more confused.'

Amr and Hussein sighed as their father looked up at his grandson's picture. It hung prominently over what the old man still considered to be the boy's bed.

'It's past my bedtime and you must have better things to do than listen to me, so I'll say goodnight,' Hag Adel said abruptly, continuing to study the picture.

'You don't usually go to bed this early, Father,' Safeya objected. 'It's not even dark.'

'I'm tired,' he explained.

His sons kissed him on the forehead before wishing him pleasant dreams.

Out in the street, Amr complained, 'He loved Hossam more than he's ever loved us, and yet we've been good sons. We have never failed to do what was expected of us.'

'Don't take it to heart,' Hussein counselled. 'Father's not as clear-headed as he believes he is. Do you think he'll really try to go to the demonstration?'

'He sounded serious, but he can't be. Old men get fixated on an idea, and then refuse to let go. Perhaps it helps them kill the time, but it certainly is trying for those around them.'

Safeya berated her father after the two men were gone. 'You're very hard on my brothers – too hard. They mean well. You should be grateful that they're concerned about your well-being.'

Hag Adel shrugged, 'I feel more comfortable in the company of young men than I do in theirs. I understand young men better.'

'You get along with your Canadian friend and he's their age,' Safeya pointed out. 'Do you really want to go to sleep right now?'

'Yes,' he said.

The next morning, Hag Adel surprised Safeya by asking her for two eggs in addition to his usual bowl of yoghurt. 'I need my strength for the demonstration,' he said.

Safeya was not sure whether he was joking. 'Whom will you go with, if my brothers don't take you there?' she asked.

'As I said, with the Canadian. I'll ask him. He's bound to pay us a visit in the next couple of days. No week goes by without him coming to see us.'

'One day, these visits will stop. He'll return to Canada.'

'I doubt it,' Hag Adel said. 'And if he does, I'll be buried by then.'

'Father, please stop saying this! What's the point? It's not in your hands anyway.' Safeya paused before asking, 'So you think that he'll be coming this week?'

I'm no fool. She enjoys his visits as much as I do, but there's no harm, her father thought. 'Yes, I do,' he answered. 'We're his only friends in Egypt.'

'But when he comes, he hardly talks. He sits downs and mostly listens to you.'

'It's not his fault if he cannot speak much Arabic, though he is learning. Besides, talking is not necessary amongst friends. Real friends can talk or not talk,' Hag Adel said. 'It should be that way between husband and wife, but it rarely is. A wife takes offence if her husband is quiet. She doesn't understand that it can be a mark of very happy companionship.'

No sooner had Hag Adel finished his sentence than he regretted talking about married life to his daughter who, at forty-five and with her limp, stood no chance of getting married. *God must want me alive for her sake* was the thought he woke up and fell asleep with these days. Tender as his feelings were towards her, he was weary of worrying about her future and feeling guilty about inevitably failing her by dying.

'Mother could be quiet,' she said with reproach in her voice.

'Not for long enough,' her father said; then to appease her, he predicted, 'Our quiet Canadian will be coming soon.'

'God willing,' Safeya said.

Stepping out of the hotel, Sam decided to stick to his plan to walk along the Corniche before going to the café and then calling in on Hag Adel and Safeya. Tomorrow he might start looking for a flat to rent, though staying at the hotel had its appeal. He liked the simplicity of the life he led there, being fussed over by the hotel manager, who was attuned to his moods and, for the most part, knew when to talk and when to leave him alone. In a flat, he risked spending days without hearing his own voice.

'Sir, don't go for a walk; it's a very bad time for walking in the city,' the hotel manager had advised, his tone more insistent than usual – a tone into which Sam had read, 'Doesn't this foreigner know any better than to be roaming around the city?'

Not wanting to seem dismissive of the warning, Sam had tried to reassure the manager by saying that he only meant to pay a visit to some friends, and that he would be taking a taxi.

What life had been like in the country before the revolution he could not imagine. He had only known it in this state of constant upheaval and had given up trying to understand the ever-changing situation. In recent days, he found himself vacillating between thinking that Morsi and the Muslim Brotherhood were being demonised, or that they probably deserved the anger directed at them.

So it was this total lack of clarity, his growing perplexity, rather than the fear of saying the wrong thing or his deficient Arabic that kept him quiet at the café whenever some of the patrons sought to draw him in a discussion. He spoke little also with Hag Adel, who did not mince his words when expressing his views. Sam had gotten used to having others do the talking. It suited him fine. Egyptians liked to talk. They talked well and, almost always, tried to make sure he could follow them.

There was nobody but him and three teenagers walking behind him in the alley. He assumed they were teenagers from the sound of their voices – young voices, male voices.

'Egyptian.'

'Not Egyptian.'

'Egyptian.'

'Not Egyptian, I tell you.'

'I bet you ten pounds he's Egyptian.'

'He doesn't walk like one.'

'We don't all walk the same. I don't walk like *you*.'

'What's wrong with how I walk?'

'Don't be so touchy! Nothing's wrong. Your trousers are tighter than mine, maybe that's why we don't walk alike.'

Sam heard two of them laugh.

'He's not Egyptian,' said the third voice, sounding irritated now.

Sam turned around and stopped. He was right. They were young, not yet over twenty he reckoned, and they looked remarkably alike. *Cousins if not brothers,* he thought. They continued to walk in his direction but at a snail's pace.

'I told you he's Egyptian,' said the tallest.

'He's not Egyptian,' the heavy, short one insisted.

'Stop arguing,' said the third teenager, winking as well as smiling at Sam.

The three youths seemed harmless, yet Sam was ill at ease. He suspected it was a mistake for him to have stopped and to be looking at them; it could be interpreted as confrontational. He was about to turn away and keep walking, but the thought that this would be a rude thing to do now that he was face-to-face with them immobilized him.

Just as Sam was about tell them that he was indeed Egyptian, the short, bulky teenager reached into his pocket and hurled a stone at him.

'Egyptian,' Sam heard himself shout before he collapsed.

'I told you he's Egyptian,' the tall teenager let out, surprise and fear on his face. As he dashed down the alley followed by the others, he yelled, '*Why* did you do that?'

'It was only a tiny pebble. He'll be fine,' the stone thrower responded, running as fast as he could.

Morsi is in jail and Mubarak is about to get out of it.

Hag Adel's son, Amr, is dead. He was shot by security forces while he was talking to supporters of Morsi demonstrating in Giza. Hag Adel's Canadian friend is dead too. He was found lying on the pavement, a gash in his head and a stone by his side, not far from the café where he used to meet Hag Adel and Hossam.

Safeya is at her wit's end. For days now, her father has asked her several times a day, 'What happened to Amr? What happened to our Canadian friend?' as though he wants to punish himself by hearing repeatedly that his son and his friend are dead.

Today she tries to reason with him. In response to his request that she recount once more how the two men died, she says, while sponging his back, 'Why do you want to torture yourself?'

'I need to hear it again,' he says.

She does not have the heart or the energy to refuse, so she narrates, once again, the terrible events. Just before she is about to end with her habitual 'It was God's will', he cuts in, 'Don't say it was God's will! It cannot have been God's will!'

'These are not good words,' she says, though without much conviction.

Ignoring her rebuke, Hag Adel repeats, 'No ya Safeya, it was not God's will.'

Marwan's Return

Marwan knew right away which key to use. After inserting it in the keyhole, he held it for a few seconds, wondering what it would feel like to walk into the apartment in which he had grown up, which he still thought of as his mother's apartment despite the building's owner claiming it as his. So many years had passed since he last stepped into the apartment. Were he alive, his brother would have fought tooth and nail to keep it. He was certain of that. He, however, had no intention of standing in the proprietor's way.

He usually avoided thinking of Ramzi, who had died young, and without having let go of the notion that his wife and his brother were attracted to each other and perhaps had even had an affair. There had been no open confrontation between them about those suspicions, no heart-to-heart talk either. But Ramzi had hinted that it would be best that he spaced out his frequent visits and refrained from dropping in on Esmeralda in his absence. Aware of Ramzi's jealousy, their mother had blamed Esmeralda for being a flirt. He had not known what to do except respect his brother's desire to see less of him, which had been hard as they had been very close. His leaving Egypt had been prompted in part by his brother's suspicions and the toll it had taken on their relationship. A couple of years after Ramzi's death,

Esmeralda had remarried. 'Esmeralda did not truly love Ramzi,' his mother had written to him. 'She loved his love and being indulged, something he did in spades, as if he owed it to her for having given up America for his sake. I will never forgive myself for encouraging him to ask her to return to Egypt and marry him. I believed that she and I were kindred spirits because we were both born in Mansoura, but I was wrong. The time she spent in America changed her. She did not come back the same girl. She was so pretty, though. The girls from Mansoura deserve their reputation as the prettiest girls in Egypt.'

Part of the lore he and Ramzi had grown up with was the fabled beauty of the girls from Mansoura and the courage and presence of mind of Shagaret el Dorr, a 13th century Sultana and the only woman ever to have ruled- if fleetingly- Islamic Egypt. 'Shagaret el Dorr was from Mansoura,' he would insist, despite his mother repeating that no, she was of Turkish origin and born in the Levant; but Mansoura could claim her for, without her, the Crusaders might not have been defeated. His mother had given her boys a watered-down account of Shagaret el Dorr's life, focusing on how this determined woman had kept the fighting spirit of the Egyptian forces alive by concealing the sudden death of her husband, the Sultan of Egypt, as he was gearing up for battle. After the Sultan's son's murder – if not at her behest, at least with her approval – Shagaret el Dorr had become Sultana of Egypt, prompting the Caliph in Baghdad to declare: 'Are there no men left in Egypt?' Pressured to take a husband, she remarried and passed the reins of powers to her new husband while remaining involved in the management of the country's affairs. When telling that tale to her wide-eyed sons, Marwan's mother would skip the crimes instigated by Shagaret el Dorr, including the murder of her second husband, and the gruesome death she met. 'Do you know what I read? Shagaret el Dorr was beaten to death with wooden clogs and then her body was left to rot for the dogs to eat,' Ramzi had recounted to Marwan around the time of Marwan's eighth birthday. 'Not true! You're a liar,' Marwan had objected, and Ramzi had walked away, retorting, 'It serves me right for thinking you're no longer a child.' For weeks after hearing that terrifying account, despite clinging to the belief that his brother was not to be trusted, Marwan had dreaded going to bed – wild dogs devouring corpses were haunting his nights. Not wanting to get Ramzi into trouble or have the awful tale confirmed, he had avoided asking his mother whether there was any truth to it. One early morning, guessing the cause of his brother's fretful sleep, Ramzi, who shared his room, had tried to comfort him, saying, 'What does it matter how Shagaret el Dorr died? What matters is that she saved Egypt, and that she got the better of the King of France. He had to pay a huge ransom and give us back Damietta to be allowed to go back to his country. Think of that!' Then, in a generous mood, Ramzi had offered, 'Let's go to Mansoura when we're older, just the two of us. I'll take you there. Mother talks a lot about it but doesn't seem keen on going there.'

The brothers never went to see their mother's home town.

The previous night, as his plane was approaching Cairo, Marwan had resolved that he must visit Mansoura during his stay in Egypt. And yet this morning, he no longer saw the point of that excursion. What had seemed so imperative to him a few hours earlier struck him as pointless. He now doubted that he would go. An immediate deterrent was last night's bombing, which had shattered the city's security directorate and several other buildings, injuring over a hundred people and killing at least a dozen. The mood in town was likely to be bleak. Besides, he might need his passport there; his had been confiscated at the airport. The officer he had been dealing with had refused to disclose the reason why. Looking sour, the man had merely stated, 'You'll get it back in due course, you'll be contacted at your hotel and will be told where and when to pick it up.' But for observing, 'How can I check in at the hotel without it?' Marwan had remained calm, much to the disappointment of the officer who was not used to such self-control and seemed to think it necessary then to issue the warning, 'It could take a while before you're contacted,' before adding grudgingly, 'I'll give you a note for your hotel.' Resisting the temptation to argue, Marwan had waited silently for the officer to write the note. 'Do you understand that you might not have your passport for quite a while?' the officer had queried, while scribbling something on a piece of paper. 'I understand,' Marwan had said, impassively. His guess was that the authorities had got wind of his desire to make a documentary on Nasser and Amer in the days preceding Amer's apparent suicide and that they disapproved of the project, imagining that it would show Egypt's military in a bad light. Would he be able to convince them that his interest did not lie in the strengths and weaknesses of Egypt's military, but in the nature of the friendship between the two men? Had Nasser simply been relieved to hear that Amer was dead? Relieved, but also sad? Had he harboured any guilty feelings? Or was he by then seeing in his old friend only treachery, bombast, and ineptness, judging him to be a different man from the one with whom he had shared youthful dreams of a free and strong Egypt?

Ten years earlier, Marwan's wife – now his ex-wife – had accused him of being cold. 'I can't take it anymore,' she had said. 'A Norwegian who finds a Middle Easterner cold, that's unusual,' he had quipped, adding fuel to her anger; she had been expecting them to have a serious conversation. 'I can't do this anymore,' she had asserted. 'If you say so,' he had conceded while calling the waiter to order another beer. 'See what I mean?' she had thrown at him. 'No, I don't,' he had retorted. To keep her from leaving – she had started gathering her belongings – he had hurried to add, 'Did I ever tell you Shagaret el Dorr's story?' She had erupted in a nervous fit of laughter before exclaiming, 'Marwan, what on earth are you thinking of?' and, after a long pause, 'Yes, you did... when we were dating.' Clutching her handbag, she had asked, 'You never offered to take me to Egypt. Why?' Though he knew it would displease her, he had given her what he thought was an honest answer, 'Because I don't put you together with Egypt, or with my life there, you'd be looking at it from the outside, it would make me feel uncomfortable, I would be watching you watching Egypt... I'm not sure I'm explaining this well, I'm sorry.' He was hoping she would understand – or at least have a glimmer of understanding. 'And why were you not keen on us having children?' she had probed further. Again, he had spoken truthfully, 'I didn't feel that I could give a child as good a childhood as the one I had,' from which she had concluded, 'So we were not good enough for a child... I was not good enough.' A week later, she had moved out and moved in with her new love. 'Why didn't you tell me that you had fallen

in love with someone else? Why all this song and dance about
my being cold, my not wanting us to have a child, my not having
taken you to Egypt?' he had written her on a postcard sent from
Greece where he had gone to lick his wounds. 'We should talk
someday,' she had emailed him. 'What for? It's all over, is it not?'
he had emailed back.

Once, his mother too had complained about his seeming cold,
saying, 'Ramzi's a difficult man, whereas you're not. But with him
one knows where one stands, one knows what he feels. With you, one
never quite knows what's in your mind or in your heart. A mother
should be able to tell what her son feels, but I often cannot read you.
You perplex me. You were different as a boy, not so inscrutable.'
Then, adopting a lighter tone, she had suggested 'You've got too
many movies in your head; this must be the problem.' He had not
bothered reminding her that he was no movie-maker, only at best
a maker of documentaries who, to make ends meet, had opened a
restaurant which left him little energy for much else.

As he entered his mother's apartment, Marwan's nose tickled
and he almost sneezed. 'Dust,' he whispered. It must have been
a while since his cousins had had the apartment cleaned. After
switching on the light, he walked down the hallway in which
he and Ramzi used to kick a soccer ball, raising the ire of their
downstairs neighbour. The hallway was even longer than he
remembered it to be. Its walls badly needed repainting. He
stopped to look at a big crack and ran his finger along it. Maybe
his ex-wife and his mother had been right about his being cold; he
was experiencing no swell of emotion, none he could describe or
put a label on. Yet he had been happy in that apartment – the three
of them had been happy, he, Ramzi and their mother. 'Happy' for

him meant that he had had time to daydream and imagine himself king of the cinema; time to feel pleasantly bored; time to fight and make up with Ramzi, the reconciliations more than compensating for the fights; time to bask in the love their mother lavished on both of them, never feeling that her love was more heavily tilted towards one or the other. Had he been blind, or naive? Or had his memory charitably buried hurt, disappointments, and bad times?

The part in us that does our living is like a stranger to us, he had read in the plane while glancing at a page of a book left open on the seat next to him; a statement he had deemed then to be pretentious nonsense. Standing in front of the cracked wall in his mother's apartment, he now thought of a possible meaning: *after we live whatever we live, we will never know it as it happened.* There was much about his life that he could not explain, much about himself that eluded him. It didn't bother him, though; he didn't believe that lives should or could be explained. At the same time, however, he would have liked to have been able to reconstruct his life exactly as it had unfolded and get all the facts right; to have been able to see it happen as one watches a movie, quite possibly exclaiming every now and then, 'Is that me? Is that really me?'

What used to be his and Ramzi's bedroom was at the very far end of the apartment, far enough from the entrance door that they would not hear a burglar breaking in, they had once teased their mother. The following day, she had put them to the test, quietly letting herself in the apartment before tiptoeing down the hallway up to their room, where they were playing a game of cards when they ought to have been tidying up. Instead of lecturing them, she had burst out laughing whereas they, mortified to be taken unawares, had grumbled that she was being silly.

Marwan headed towards his bedroom, thinking back to the days when, on returning home from school, he would go straight to his room and throw his bag on his bed before running to the kitchen in search of some snack; he was always famished after school.

As he neared the bedroom, he noticed that the door was ajar. His steps quickened, he could hear a light snore. Sound asleep, fully clothed and with lips slightly parted, a young man occupied his bed. Strange that he should still think of the bed as his, but he did.

The young man had not bothered removing the bedcover on which he lay on his stomach, face towards the door.

Not daring to enter the room lest he disturb its young occupant, Marwan remained in the doorway, noticing that, but for the bedcovers on the two beds, nothing had changed since he had been a little boy. The walls were still grey, though now a dirty grey.

The young man stirred and, as though throwing a punch at an assailant, he swung an arm, shouting, 'Don't get any closer!' He then woke up with a start and jumped out of bed. 'What's going on?' he stammered on seeing Marwan.

'I'm your uncle, ya Tarek,' Marwan said gently, as he switched on the light and stepped into the room. 'Last time you saw me, you were three, you look very much like your father, more so now than when you were three.'

Tarek tucked his shirt in his trousers. 'My uncle Marwan,' he said pensively and stood still.

It occurred to Marwan that he ought to be giving his nephew a hug, but it was too late for that – the embrace would seem contrived, and besides, he felt intimidated by the young man's somber expression. So he too stood still.

'You've come for the apartment?' Tarek said.

'The apartment?' Marwan asked.

'To make sure the building's owner does not get his hands on it,' Tarek said, sounding hostile.

His nephew's tone dismayed Marwan. 'That's not why I'm here. As far as I'm concerned, the proprietor can have the apartment.' He hesitated briefly before adding, 'But if you want it, it's another matter.'

'So what brings you to Egypt? Now is a strange time to be reconnecting with Egypt. You're not going to see it in its best light.' Tarek sounded weary now.

'But let's sit down, somewhere,' Marwan suggested. 'Let's go out for coffee. The apartment is not so inviting. It has a stuffy smell.' He decided not to ask his nephew why he happened to be in the apartment, sleeping late in the morning with his clothes on.

'I'd rather stay in, I'm a wanted man,' Tarek said as he ran his fingers nervously through his hair.

'A wanted man? How come?' Marwan exclaimed. 'But do let us sit down, preferably in the dining room. I'm more comfortable on hard chairs than in soft armchairs.'

'What's wrong with your leg? You're limping,' Tarek observed as they walked towards the dining room.

'My hip thinks I'm older than I am,' Marwan joked. 'I need a new one.'

'I gather you haven't been here for long,' Marwan said to his nephew as they sat around the dining room table, after struggling with the windows, which would not open at first; the handles were rusty and one of the wooden shutters was broken.

'Only since last night,' Tarek said.

'Can I make myself useful, be of some help?' Marwan asked.

'No, but thank you,' Tarek said. 'I doubt they'll come looking for me here.' Once again, he ran his fingers through his hair. 'But perhaps you would rather stay out of this altogether. Perhaps you would like me to leave,' he offered.

'Of course not, you can stay here as long as you want. I'll make sure the building's owner does not come knocking at the door. But who are they? What's the trouble?'

'It's simple. There's no room to breathe in this country. It used to be bad, and it has gotten worse – hard to believe that it could get worse, but it has. I was having tea at my usual *ahwa*, reading an article portraying the Muslim Brotherhood as terrorists that need to be crushed. I'm no lover of the Brotherhood and never will be; I had my fights with them at university, both before and after Morsi became president. But fair is fair; they're human beings like us, and they have their supporters. I said so, out loud, and people heard me. The following evening, the waiter at the *ahwa* took me aside to let me know that two men had interrogated the *ahwa's* owner and gotten my home address, so I'd better make myself scarce for the next few days. Welcome to a country in which one had hopes that have been so thoroughly dashed that one comes to doubt one ever had them. Was it all a fantasy? We lived in the clouds for a while. Now we can clearly see what's on the horizon, and it's frightening.' Tarek shook his head and then asked, his voice flat, 'What made you decide to come, if it isn't the apartment? It can't be tourism.'

'No, not tourism, though there's much of Egypt I don't know – a bit of touring around wouldn't hurt me. I have come to do some research on a subject that has been a life-long interest of mine: the friendship between Nasser and Amer; how it changed with both of them wanting power.'

'Why bother?' Tarek said bluntly.

'You think it's a worthless project?"

'Nasser… Amer, if you don't mind my saying so, all this is yesterday. And yesterday is a luxury we can't afford right now.'

'It's the future we should be thinking of?'

'The present, *today,* is what we should be thinking of! Not yesterday, not tomorrow. I'm sorry if I'm offending you; I don't mean to.'

'Not to worry – I appreciate your frankness.'

'My father was an army man. I want to believe that he'd have been saddened by the turn of events, but maybe I'm wrong, maybe he would be cheering for Sisi. My memories of him are vague and getting vaguer. On whose side would he have been, do you think?'

'I haven't seen you since you were a little boy who couldn't even reach the table, and here we are talking only about politics. How about you, Tarek? How have things been with you? Did you go to university?'

'So you think that my father would have approved of what Sisi is doing?'

'You're not going to let me off the hook, are you? I honestly don't know. I lost touch with Egypt.'

'You lost touch with my father too, after you left Egypt, didn't you? Well, I don't mean to say that you were totally out of touch, but you were no longer as close as you had been once, isn't that the case?'

The question stung Marwan. He avoided answering it. 'Yes, we were very close,' he said.

Tarek hung his head and stated, 'It must be hard for you to be back and not have him around.' Still looking down, he continued, 'What can I tell you about my life? I'm a lawyer and I don't have much of a job, though my stepfather did his best to find me one through his connections.' Now, raising his head and with an air of profound disillusionment, he carried on, 'I was engaged not so long ago… but she broke it off; she decided that I would never be in a position to support us in the style she's accustomed to, and she was probably right in that regard. She also didn't like my politics – she considered me too much of an idealist.'

'Do you still love her?'

'I would be a fool if I did.'

'Do you sometimes think of leaving Egypt?'

'I should. Sisi and the likes of him would love to rid the country of men like me. But we're not going anywhere. We'll stay. They'll have to deal with us.'

Seeming to have run out of things to say to each other, the two men fell silent until Tarek inquired, 'Are you planning to get in touch with my mother?'

Startled, Marwan, faltered, 'I… I wasn't… why do you ask?'

'I heard that you were in love with her, and that that was the reason you and my father grew apart,' Tarek stated without looking at Marwan. Then he rose, went over to the window and looked out.

'People talk a lot in Egypt – that's one thing Egyptians excel in. Suppose it were true though, why should it matter? More than thirty years have passed since I left Egypt. Your mother remarried, and I hope for her sake and yours that her husband is a good man.'

Tarek turned around and, fixing his eyes on his uncle as though sizing him up, he declared, 'I'm more interested in that past than in Nasser and Amer. You're right, however; it's not so important. My stepfather is a good man, a decent man.'

'I'm glad to hear that,' said Marwan. 'That's what your father would have wanted for your mother.'

'My grandmother used to say that you were a hard man to read.'

Marwan smiled. 'Did she? What else did she say about me? Mothers are supposed to praise their children, not to draw attention to their failings. Back to you, though – I'm concerned about you. When do you think it will be safe for you to be going about your usual business?'

Tarek shrugged. 'My guess is as good as yours. I'm waiting to see what happens in the next couple of days, whether they go looking for me at home. The waiter, who by the way is sympathetic to the Brotherhood, might have overstated the matter.'

Marwan frowned. 'The least I can do is to get you some food, or take you out for lunch somewhere close to here.'

'Let's meet for dinner. For lunch, I'll ask the bawab to get me some *ful* sandwiches.'

'You're sure?'

'I'm sure.'

'I hate the thought of you spending the day all by yourself in this dusty apartment.'

'Infinitely better than spending it in jail,' said Tarek. 'Don't worry; I have phone calls to make. I'll be resting some more. I didn't sleep much last night.'

Marwan sensed that Tarek wanted him to leave, so after they had agreed on meeting for dinner at a nearby restaurant he told the young man that he had a few errands to do in town. He walked out of the apartment feeling that this first encounter with his nephew had not gone well.

The old anger he had kept locked within himself was surfacing and taking hold of him, anger at his dead brother for having made a mess of things with his suspicious mind.

He retreated to his hotel, went straight to his room, hung the 'Do Not Disturb' sign on door and then sat on the balcony facing the Nile. As he gazed at the water seeking to regain some equanimity, his anger, rather than receding, grew. If his brother were alive, he would give him a piece of his mind. He would say to him, 'Yes, I fancied Esmeralda a bit, but that was without any consequence other than that I enjoyed being around her. It was only after it became clear that you were all in a knot about it, after I stayed away to respect your wishes, that it grew into something more, and then it came to feel like love. Your unease, your desire that I see less of her roused the very feelings you feared I had – before you made your displeasure known, my feelings for her were warm; after that, while I hardly saw her and certainly never just by myself, I found myself falling in love with her. You bear that responsibility. In hindsight, perhaps that was what you had wanted, my falling in love with an unattainable object, for how could you have imagined that I would woo – let alone sleep with – your wife? Thanks to you, I have become a foreigner in my country. I left because of you, I left to give you peace of mind and try to get Esmeralda out of my mind.'

Was this really what had happened? He could imagine what his brother's riposte would be. 'Fabulist! You're making a movie out of your life! Get real!' Ramzi would no doubt have retorted.

Suddenly, his mind was brimming with unpleasant scenes: Ramzi describing to him with seeming relish Shagaret El Dorr's death; Ramzi pinning him to the ground to demonstrate his unquestioned physical superiority; Ramzi yelling at him 'You're mad!' for pursuing an unknown woman at Café Astra on that saddest of days, the day Nasser resigned in acknowledgement of the army's rout.

'What's the matter with me?' Marwan whispered, his anger dissolving into some inchoate sadness.

He saw no point in getting in touch with Esmeralda; he would prefer not to meet her. He would of course like to remember her forever young. But mostly, he did not want to read in her eyes the inevitable 'What have you made of your life?' to which he could answer no more than 'I have just lived it.'

He got up and went to lie down, hoping he could fall asleep. He wanted to dream. His Shagaret el Dorr nightmares aside, he was blessed with a pleasurable dream life. He was blessed with the kind of dreams that made one wish for more sleep on waking up in order to dream some more.

He was too wide awake to fall asleep. As he lay very still in bed, a surprising idea began to take shape in his mind – he must find the woman with whom he had ended up spending the night the evening Nasser had resigned, the woman who, on seeing him cry, had given him her handkerchief. The more he thought about it, the more he felt he ought to find her and thank her for her kindness. Upon leaving her flat stealthily at dawn, he had promised himself to return to express his gratitude. But once he was home, it had seemed to him that another meeting might spoil the memory of his night with her. That had been his justification for not paying her another visit. All these years later, he could truthfully say that sex for him would never again be quite as intense as that first time when a woman, heartbroken over Nasser's resignation and her country's bitter defeat, had drowned her sorrow by comforting him.

Soraya was her name. He had not forgotten it. And he could still picture her miniscule apartment on the ground floor of a building right behind Café Astra – an ancient building with a magnificent cast iron door, but in a state of great disrepair in 1967. Claiming the apartment to be hers, she had explained, 'It was my grandfather's. I lived with him, but he died ten years ago, God bless his soul. I was the apple of his eye. There could not have been a better grandfather.' Of mother or father she made no mention. If she was still alive, she would be well into her seventies.

He could go, take a look at the building and try to find out what had become of her, perhaps even knock at her door. He could do that now; there was no reason to wait.

After the taxi driver dropped him off in front of the French Lycée, he had no trouble locating the building, which, from the outside, looked no worse than it had in 1967. The alley facing it was filthy and was being used, in effect, as a parking lot. In between the lines of cars clogging it as well as its narrow footpaths, young boys were kicking a soccer ball. Marwan marvelled at how anybody could drive a car in or out of that alley.

He slowly made his way to the building and then stopped right in front of it, facing the small balcony that extended out of the ground floor apartment where he had spent that extraordinary night. Whoever now lived in the apartment had succeeded in wedging a chair onto it. Hearing giggles, Marwan looked up. One floor above, two young girls were hanging laundry. They were not laughing at him. They were not even looking at him. It made him feel his age.

Standing was hard on his hip, but he lingered. The girls had finished hanging their laundry. Leaning against their balcony railing, they seemed to be confiding secrets to one another.

He was about to circle the building to give himself some time to consider what to do next when, supported by a cane, an old, short and heavy-set woman walked onto the tiny balcony of the ground floor apartment. She sat down and gave a heavy sigh. Her hair was covered by a hijab, her body by a long, loose robe. She was wearing large sunglasses. Her jowly face was remarkably unlined. Though the sunglasses made it difficult to really tell, Marwan saw no trace of Soraya in that face.

'Are you looking for someone?' the elderly woman asked.

He looked at her face again, the voice sounded familiar. It had the gravelly quality of Soraya's voice.

'Soraya Hanem?' he ventured to ask.

'What can I do for you?' she asked. 'I only work in the evenings.'

Nonplussed, he nevertheless suggested, 'I can come back.'

'How did you hear about me?' she quizzed him.

'Through a friend of a friend,' he said.

She smiled. 'Your friend's friend must have been satisfied with my services.'

'Of course,' he said, sensing mockery in her observation.

'I do make exceptions and see people during the day sometimes,' she said. 'I would hate for you to have to come back.

You seem uncomfortable. At our age, our legs don't support us all too well.' She laughed.

Marwan no longer had any doubts. The woman was Soraya. That laugh was unmistakably hers. Despite their sadness, they had laughed that night for which he had come to thank her. Big, yet at the same time soft, her laugh was unchanged.

Soraya stood up and invited him in, saying, 'It will take longer than it ought to for me to get to the door. Patience is another thing we must learn at our age.'

'What work could she be possibly doing?' went through his mind. Then, 'She considers me old, even though I must be at least ten years younger than her.' Walking towards the entrance door, he made a conscious effort to limp less.

From upstairs, the girls threw a 'Welcome, ya Uncle' at him.

The first thing Soraya Hanem told him upon opening the door was, 'You must be prepared to drink two cups of coffee, for I always do two readings. Two cups give me a fuller picture.' While leading him to the sitting room, she stated, perhaps to test him, 'Your friend's friend must have explained to you how I proceed. Did he tell you that the fee is up to the customer? If they don't like what they hear, they don't need to pay.' Chuckling, she mentioned having had only one customer who had refused to pay.

Had he changed so much that she had no idea who he was? Had that night been of so little importance to her that it had left her with no lasting impression? Or was she waiting for him to allude to their night together? Marwan did not know what to think.

The apartment was bursting with furniture and bric-a-brac. She had filled it up since that night.

Sitting on a settee covered with shiny, gold fabric, he waited for Soraya Hanem to return with the promised cups of coffee. He did not usually drink Turkish coffee, but when he did, he liked it sugarless.

Unaided by her cane, she entered the room, carrying a tray on which two cups and a coffee pot rested. She put the tray down on a table near the settee. 'There's no sugar in the coffee,' she announced. For a moment, he wondered whether he had had sugarless coffee that one night, and she was tacitly saying to him, 'You see, I haven't forgotten.' But that was not it, as she proceeded to explain, 'I can't do a proper reading with sugar in the coffee.'

She had not removed her glasses. 'My eyes are tired, that's why I'm wearing these dark glasses,' she said, settling in an overstuffed armchair within reach of the settee. 'I'll remove them when I do the reading,' she hastened to add and then remarked, 'It's so good to take one's weight off one's feet, particularly when there's too much of it.'

Once again, the sound of her laughter delighted him.

'I'm not here for you tell me what is awaiting me in the future; I'd rather not know. There's not that much future, ahead of me anyways,' he said in order to say something, anything.

'Don't say that! You don't know; it could be days, weeks, months or years... by the way, when I do my readings, I never disclose that information, even if I can clearly see a person's lifeline in the cup. It's a rule I am not prepared to relax. Back to you though, is it that you want to know what the future holds for a loved one? One of your children?'

'I have no children,' he said tersely. To his ears, it sounded strangely like an admission of guilt.

'Neither have I,' she said before pouring him a cup of coffee.

A couple of swigs and he had finished it.

'It's still very hot, and it's not good for you to drink it that hot,' she said while pouring coffee in the second cup.

He drained the second cup as fast as he had the first.

She deftly turned the cups upside down and then placed them on their respective saucers. 'So whose future do you want to know? Tell me, then let's be quiet for a while. I need to concentrate while the coffee grounds settle. As for you, try to empty your mind of all thoughts. I'll close my eyes while we wait. You can do the same.'

'It's the future of Egypt that interests me,' he said.

'Are you a politician?' she said, sounding serious. 'Quite a few pay me regular visits, but they come for personal reasons.'

He laughed. 'No, no, I'm not a politician,' he said. 'I'm just a regular Egyptian who wants to know where his country's heading.'

'Remember when we lost the war and Nasser resigned and we were inconsolable, fearing the worst,' she reminisced.

'*She probably knows who I am,*' Marwan thought, very much hoping she did. 'Yes, I remember,' he said. 'Of course I do!'

'The country is too sore a subject for me to contemplate,' she declared, her voice harshening. Then she stated, gently though, 'You have come here for a reason. Tell me what brought you here.'

'The past,' he said.

'I can read the future, but not the past', she said. 'So you need to tell me more.'

'I'm sorry to have come empty-handed,' he said out of the blue, ashamed not to have brought her a present.

'There's no need for you to feel sorry. Shall we forget about the reading?' she offered. 'It seems to me that your heart is not in it.'

'Another time,' he said.

'Will there be another time?' she queried aloud. As though narrating a story to a child, she then began reciting, 'Long ago, I met a young man, a very young man,' at which point she broke off without elaborating.

By now convinced that she knew who he was, he said, 'You see, you can read the past.'

'Hardly,' she said.

He reached out for her hand and pressed it.

'Too much is being said about that poor country of ours! Words, words, and yet more words!' she stated angrily.

'You're right,' he agreed, while holding her hand.

'All those years back, we were full of anguish, but we had not lost hope – not entirely. How about today's youth? Are they still hopeful?' she pondered.

He thought of his nephew Tarek, who seemed utterly dejected but was not prepared to leave the country and so must be clinging to some hope. Then he thought of her, Soraya Hanem, the fortune teller, the old woman sitting beside him, whose hand he was holding.

'Since you say that you're not good at reading the past, let me shed some light on it; let me tell you something that's very important for me to say, to say to you – I'm immensely grateful to you.' The words flew out of his mouth. He had not had to think of what to say.

'I was in love then, madly in love,' she said.

'Really?' he breathed, vaguely disappointed.

'How is your brother?' she asked.

Her question confounded him. He released her hand. Had she known Ramzi? Had she been in love with Ramzi?

Guessing what was going through his mind, she revealed, 'I knew your brother. He had set you up with my young friend. He used to talk about you, he even told us how upset you were, as a young child, to hear that Shagaret el Dorr was beaten to death. He regretted having upset you. He used to say that you meant the world to him. You must be asking yourself questions about us. I mean about him and me. We never slept together. And you know why? Because he knew how crazy I was about him, how ready I was to do anything for him; he did not want to break my heart. That was the sort of man he was. There were not too many like your brother. He was younger than I was but infinitely wiser.'

Was she telling him the truth? Or being kind?

'How is he?' she asked again.

He could not get himself to tell her.

She cried, 'Ramzi dead… How can that be?'

Her words hit him hard. He blurted out, 'And I wasn't even there when he died!'

Seconds later, after wiping her cheeks, she handed him her handkerchief.

Escape

On their way to the airport, Habiba said, 'Sometimes, I get the feeling you create drama in order to get some writing material, or when inspiration deserts you.'

Fuad did not bother defending himself. He merely smiled and suddenly remembered that the euros he had been looking for were in his sock drawer. He was used to forgetting where he had put things. Even as a child, he had been forgetful, his parents would despair, observing that he had too much trivia on his mind for there to be any room left for what was really important. Though long-standing and, therefore, not a sign of age, his forgetfulness now troubled him, whereas it never had in the past.

'Don't worry about Ali, I'll take good care of him,' Habiba said.

He was quite worried about Ali who had been talking less of late and seemed morose at times. 'He's our age, reason enough to be concerned,' he remarked. 'Ali and I have been through practically everything together.'

'Will we ever get to the airport?' Habiba muttered.

Hunched over the wheel, clutching it as if it were a life buoy, the taxi driver was steering erratically at a snail's speed even though there was hardly any traffic. The sun was yet to rise. It crossed Fuad's mind that the driver, who was old and wearing thick glasses, had trouble seeing. Feeling sorry for the man, he decided not to complain. But then, just as a car ahead of them had come to a stop, the driver sped up. 'Careful! Can you not see?' Fuad exclaimed.

Slowing down, the driver retorted, 'Have no fear, we're in God's hands.'

'In yours too!' Fuad bemoaned.

Seconds later, at an intersection, the driver seemed unaware of an oncoming bus on his left. Once again, God was merciful, the near collision did not materialise. By now convinced that the man was nearly blind, Fuad thought it pointless to protest. He said nothing even when they went right over a pothole and a spasm shot through his lower back. Habiba, on the other hand, heatedly berated the driver, who ignored her.

'It's all right, it's all right,' Fuad said, trying to calm her down.

She had insisted on accompanying him to the airport, though his plane was leaving hours before she normally got out of bed. He was thankful for her presence, since he could not rule out being arrested or at least stopped from leaving the country. It would be good to have her there just in case.

She was his cousin and, fifty-five years earlier, had been his wife for a mere ten months, at the end of which they had agreed that they were too young to while away their nights in tepid embraces. Forming a united front and without providing any details, they had told their two sets of bemused parents that their feelings for each other were not strong enough to sustain a marriage, they had believed themselves to be more in love than they were. After all, they were only eighteen! She had become the friend whom he knew he could always count on, though they did not see eye-to-eye often, and she could exasperate him with her sensible remarks and her do-gooding. At times, he was ashamed of himself for taking her as much for granted as he did. At other times, he found her company burdensome and barely paid attention to what she said. Then, the thought and the hope that she probably felt the same about him afforded him some comfort, assuaging his bad conscience for treating her more like a fixture in his life than the friend she had become. If asked what he thought of her, he would have said, 'She's a very good sort, a gem, really.' But would he or could he have said that he really enjoyed her company? For both of them, their marriage had been a prelude to more mistakes – another two failed marriages each. They were single now. Scattered across continents so too far away to be of any real help to their parents, her children and his were urging them to get back together. But they were not the slightest bit tempted.

Was he doing the right thing to be leaving the country after being warned by a well-connected acquaintance that his latest article had angered the authorities? That he had overstepped the 'acceptable boundaries' of free speech? Habiba believed he was overreacting, as his acquaintance was known to be an exaggerator and an alarmist. When informed of his intention to leave, she had pointed out that, not so long ago, he would have ignored the warning; age must have something to do with his reaction. Not that she wanted him to continue criticizing the regime; she in fact supported its heavy-handed approach. She thought that, in the current circumstances, it had no choice but to use an iron fist. She failed to understand why he did not appreciate the mortal danger the Islamists posed. The democratic forces had had their chance and squandered it and that was that! In her view, he was an old dreamer with unrealistic expectations who would be well advised to keep his thoughts to himself, though not because he might incur the wrath of the authorities, but because he had poor judgment. Besides, the thought that fear was driving him away did not sit well with her. In any case, was he not giving himself more importance than was due? Surely, a lone, old writer sounding off, a writer with as limited a readership as he had, could not be foremost on the regime's mind. She had told him all this and more – she had not minced her words – and yet she was willing to accompany him to the airport. And to look after Ali! The reserved, bashful girl of his youth had metamorphosed into an outspoken woman with strong opinions and a strongly held faith. Very few people knew how deeply religious she was, that she had gone on pilgrimage to Mecca more than once. Her faith was a matter she kept to herself. To this day, she and Fuad had never discussed the central role religion played in her life. During their short-lived marriage, it had not taken him long to discover the significance she attached to religion. Invoking some excuse or other, she would discreetly disappear from the room to go and pray; if offered a drink, she would quietly decline it; and the one Ramadan they had spent together, she had managed to make fasting seem easy. She wore her religion so lightly that he had not minded this unexpected side of her.

'What are you going to do about your aunt's apartment?' Habiba asked him. 'Will you continue to let Amira live in it?'

'How can I not?' he said. 'She cared for my aunt, who wasn't easy to look after, not even in good health. Amira was a mere girl when she left her village to work for my aunt, who virtually raised her – she taught her how to read and write. They became indispensable to each other over the years. You know that history. I couldn't turf Amira out.'

'I understand, I would feel the same,' Habiba said. 'However, there's an issue that concerns me. Rumour has it that the apartment is now in Amira's name. Perhaps it ought to be, given her relationship to your aunt. It'd only be fair. But you can well imagine the complications arising if her brothers get wind of that! They'll want that apartment; they'll find a way to get their hands on it.'

'I doubt that she has much to do with them – it's been years since she's seen them, years since she's been back in her village; and as I recall, her last visit there was disastrous. She had a big fight with her brothers,' Fuad said.

'Precisely! There's not much love between the brothers and their sister, she didn't grow up with them. Surely, they must envy her material comfort. The moment they know the apartment's in her name, they'll wish her dead, and who knows what might happen?'

'You don't mean to say that they'll get rid of her?' Fuad said.

'It's quite possible,' Habiba said.

'Who's the dramatist now?' Fuad said and laughed.

'This is no joking matter, *ya* Fuad. Is the apartment in her name?'

'Yes,' he said.

'That wasn't a wise thing to do,' Habiba deplored before predicting, 'With you gone, her brothers may descend on her. She would be at their mercy, and what I have heard about them doesn't fill me with confidence. If I were you, I'd be far more worried about what may happen to Amira than to what may happen to Ali in your absence.'

'But tell me, how will the brothers know that I'm gone? And who is going to tell them that the apartment's in her name?' Fuad wondered.

'News gets around, my dear,' Habiba said. 'Rest assured it does.'

'Amira is a force of nature. She'll know how to deal with them if they knock at her door, which is highly unlikely,' Fuad said.

'You're an optimist. No wonder your political analysis is wrong-headed,' Habiba lamented.

'So why am I leaving if I'm such an optimist?'

She smiled, but barely. Then she surprised him by asking, 'What's your opinion about what's happening in Yemen? Are we going to get bogged down in the mire of a war there? I'd have thought that we learnt that lesson. Nasser's war in Yemen cost him a great deal. It definitely contributed to us losing the war in 1967; we were spread too thin. He and the Saudis were on opposite sides then. Now, we'd be allies. He would find that hard to believe.'

'I'm with you on that one. Fighting in Yemen is a bad idea,' Fuad said, without sounding overly interested in pursuing that discussion.

'What's Yemen to us?' the driver chimed in.

'At least he's not deaf,' went through Fuad's mind.

Habiba continued, 'And what should one make of the fact that here, supporters of the Muslim Brotherhood are against us fighting in Yemen, whereas the Muslim Brotherhood in Yemen is *for* an intervention?'

'Why should that be surprising? It's politics. You can't expect politics to make sense,' the driver butted in before adding, 'that's why I don't vote, that's why I want nothing to do with protests, demonstrations, revolutions of whatever sort, I don't believe in change, nothing ever really changes. You don't need to be a student of history to reach that conclusion. Change means a new set of politicians, nothing more. It's still politics, and what politicians do is play with people's lives – not change them for the better. And it doesn't matter whether they're civilian or military, Brothers or not. For the politicians, the people are merely pieces on a board, to use and to abuse. You and I can talk about politics and speculate about this and that but it's just talk that'll get us nowhere. As far as I'm concerned, all that matters is earning one's livelihood; all the rest is clouds in the sky.'

'You have a point, but you're taking it a bit further than I would,' Habiba told the unexpectedly communicative driver.

'We're near the airport,' Fuad said, much relieved that the discussion would soon come to an end.

'Pardon me for giving advice on a subject that's no business of mine – I couldn't help but hear your exchange of views. If I were you, I'd be concerned about the brothers of this lady Amira,' the driver stated.

'Thank you! I'll have plenty of time during the flight to mull this over,' Fuad said, grateful to the driver for steering the conversation away from the subject of politics. He was so very tired of that subject, tired of Egypt, tired of thinking in circles about what had gone wrong, about what could have happened, what should be done now and how the situation was likely to unfold. In truth, he was not leaving because he was afraid. Habiba was right that they were unlikely to come after him; he was too old and too marginal for them to bother with. For a brief while after hearing his acquaintance's warning he had been alarmed, but that had passed. He was no longer afraid. He was leaving because he had nothing more to say, his mind had grown sterile, he was repeating himself, he had become disconnected from the words he wrote. He found it increasingly difficult to compose even a single page and yet could not bear the thought of being in Egypt without writing. That was the real reason he was leaving. How to begin explaining any of this to Habiba? Much better to let her believe that fear, rather than an empty head, was driving him away.

When they arrived at the airport, she got out of the taxi to bid him farewell. It had been years since family and friends could walk in and wave their goodbyes to the passengers heading towards the gates. Only passengers were allowed to enter the airport now.

'Call us! Email us!' Habiba said. 'Don't forget us in Paris. If you do, I'll hop on a plane and come to see you – to remind you of us!'

'You make it sound like a threat,' he said.

To his utter surprise, she came out with, 'Sometimes I get the feeling you don't like my company. You listen to me without interacting much.' Her tone was not reproachful though.

He hastened to reassure her by saying what was in part true, 'It's my own company – my own self – I like less and less. Do come to Paris. We'll have fun.'

'Fun at our age? You really are an optimist.'

He chuckled.

'Seriously, we'll miss you,' Habiba said, 'Ali will miss you very much. I'll do my best to keep him happy and healthy.'

Was he ever going to return to Egypt? Would he ever see Ali again? The desire to explain to Habiba why he was leaving – the hollowness he felt, the sterility of his thoughts, his sudden mental lethargy – came over him. But there was not enough time.

While hugging him, she said, 'Your parrot will be fine, I know how much Ali means to you, I'll make sure he keeps talking… as long as he doesn't follow in his master's footsteps and say things that would force him into exile.'

Since his arrival in Paris, Fuad had his morning coffee on Rambuteau, a mere ten-minute walk from the building where he resided in an apartment a childhood friend had lent him. The friend had decided he much preferred living on a boat in Sicily to breathing Paris' polluted air.

Every day on his way to the café, right around the corner of his building, Fuad went past an old homeless woman who, unless she was asleep, invariably demanded, 'Hey you, hey you, give me twenty euros!' and on occasion, insisted, 'You can afford to give me those twenty euros, you know!' She uttered those commands either fully stretched out on the pavement or sitting on it with her back leaning against the front window of a grocery store that sold organic foods. Surrounded by rubbish, scraps of paper, stacks of magazines in cardboard boxes, and garbage bags overflowing with her belongings, she had converted that spot into her living quarters. Once in a while, rivalling her in filth, a young man sat or slept by her side. Whenever he saw that youth, Fuad wondered whether they were related. Her son? Her grandson?

The first time Fuad had walked by her, he had not had the slightest inclination to reach into his pocket. Her manner was so off-putting, so preposterous; and she looked so repulsive! A glimpse of her had been enough for him to quicken his step and avert his eyes. He could have chosen to go a different way to the café after this initial encounter, but he stuck to the same course and came to admire the woman for demanding rather than begging. Nonetheless, he never once gave her money. It seemed to him that her objective was to make a statement and ruffle passers-by rather than to get money. At least that was what he told himself to justify not giving her any. He would have bet that anything less than a twenty euro bill she would throw back at him.

She was toothless and shoeless. In sharp contrast to her yellowing nails, the soles of her feet were black, the shrivelled skin around her ankles was leather-like, her oily, thinning grey hair hung in clumps around her shoulders. Some days, she used her hair as a curtain, covering much of her face with it. But even on those days, when Fuad walked by her and she was awake, from behind the hair came the request for twenty euros. Never less, never more.

On weekdays, close to a busy intersection further down the street, standing erect and hardly ever moving, an elderly gentleman accosted passers-by, timidly asking them if they could spare a euro. Apparently treating this activity as a regular, full-time job, he wore a kind of uniform: always the same blue suit, a white shirt and a tie and, depending on the weather, a grey raincoat. His neat appearance seemed to belie need. Yet, to him, even though he did not find him particularly likable, Fuad did give some change every now and then. Over time, that man must have gotten more than twenty euros out of him.

Already four months had passed since his arrival in Paris, but he still had much of the city to explore. At the outset, he had wandered exclusively in his neighbourhood before gradually venturing into others. He had the good fortune of still having reasonably vigorous legs and feet, and made it a rule to spend time in a neighbourhood before reading its description in the guidebooks. His eyes and ears were his first guide.

Besides strolling in the streets, he listened to music, went to the cinema, and met with the few friends he had in Paris. For the first time in his life, he read relatively little because reading made him think of his writing days, of which he would rather not be reminded. He had yet to get used to the idea that he would never write again. As he had yet to get used to the idea that he would no longer try to analyse Egypt, no longer try to make sense of what was happening there. He had reached the conclusion that he had been a cheat all along, pretending he knew his country when in fact he did not.

Habiba had announced her visit, assuring him that Ali was well and would be looked after in her absence, so he need not worry. He was apprehensive at the thought of seeing her. She was bound to talk about Egypt a great deal. She would undoubtedly ask him *when* he planned to return, not if he planned to return. In her last email, she had begun probing – albeit indirectly – by saying that, surely, he could not afford to stay in Paris forever.

Having overslept, he was late getting to the café that morning. Both Suzanne and Sabine – two of the café's regulars – were already there by the time he walked in. He normally arrived before they did. Fuad knew the two women's names from hearing the café owner address them. He had never seen them interact with one another, nor had either ever interacted with him. The three of them had come to acknowledge each other with quick nods and small smiles, hardly an invitation for closer interaction. He was surprised, then, to see the two women sitting together and engaged in an animated conversation. Suzanne, his contemporary, virtually lived in the café; the owner, a Frenchman of Algerian origin, treated her with affection. As a smoker, she was often seated at a table outside. But she also had her special table inside, where she left pads of paper, assorted pens and pencils, erasers and pencil sharpeners. She seldom wrote, though. Fuad could not picture her young; could not tell whether she had been attractive, unattractive, or simply plain. Now she looked bland: a pale face without an ounce of make-up, not even to give some definition to her almost non-existent eyebrows; white hair loosely gathered in a sloppy chignon; nondescript clothes in keeping with the image she conveyed of a woman utterly unconcerned about her appearance. Like Suzanne, but half her age, Sabine also came across as uninterested in her looks. The baggy trousers and ample sweaters she wore accentuated her tiny, androgynous build. Her crew cut suggested she let a barber chop her hair. Her face was interesting in its severity, but it kept one at a distance. During the one hour she typically spent at the café, she typed virtually nonstop.

'To condemn him to death… that really is a bit much,' he heard Suzanne exclaim as he was waiting for his coffee at the counter.

'They're discussing the latest news from Egypt,' the café owner explained and, shaking his head, he went on to say, 'Morsi has been sentenced. He got the death penalty. So did many others. For being too close to Hamas and Hezbollah – that's the allegation. These Arab rulers never fail to disappoint one. The death penalty! What for? And with what consequence? Do they ever ask themselves that question?'

Had the café owner guessed that he was from Egypt?

'Suzanne grew up in Egypt, but her family had to leave in 1956. Like all the other Jewish families. She's desperately wanted to go back, she was all set to go then the revolution started. Sabine is a journalist who spent the first two years of the revolution in Cairo. They clearly feel connected to the country, which is why they're so worked up,' the café owner opined. 'May I ask you if you're from that part of the world? Unfortunately, it's not a part of the world you can be proud of nowadays. Such a shame, such a great shame,' he sighed while serving him his coffee. Then he pondered, 'I can't help but ask myself what would have happened to the region, had Egypt not been so badly defeated in '67. Egypt losing the war in the manner it did may have unleashed the destructive forces the world is confronting today. And is Israel itself really better off for winning as conclusively as it did? A more mixed outcome might have been preferable for all parties concerned, in the long run.'

Fuad let it slip that he was 'from Egypt, actually', not realising that, about to order another cup of coffee, Sabine was standing next to him. 'From Egypt!' she cried out. 'We've just been talking about Morsi's sentence. Today's news is so unexpected.'

Intending to remain silent, Fuad could not, however, hold back. 'Really? So unexpected?' he said with an ironic inflection.

Not put off, the young woman asked eagerly, 'Can I interview you?'

'Thank you, but I don't think so. I would have nothing to say that could be of interest to anybody.'

Sabine persisted. 'When were you last in Egypt?' she asked.

'A few months ago.'

Also with them now was Suzanne, who inquired, 'I wonder whether you went to the Lycée Francais in Cairo.'

'You guessed right,' he said, wishing he had evaded the question.

'So did I!' she declared, then speculating, 'Perhaps we were in the same class.'

He responded with a non-committal, 'Our paths may have crossed.' He was aware of being unnecessarily standoffish but, if that was the way to cut short the conversation, so be it!

'I'm sorry! I can appreciate your lack of appetite for nostalgic reminiscences. This is hardly the time to be evoking the past,' she said.

'Would you care to join us?' Sabine suggested. 'I can't figure out what the regime's calculations are, whether it really wants to see Morsi hung.'

'Let's sit down,' Suzanne said.

He could not refuse, followed them to their table, and was struck by the distinctive way Suzanne moved, as though she was unsure of her step. He now recognised her: Suzanne, his classmate and rival, they had competed for prizes in all the important subjects. He had breathed a sigh of relief when she was gone, being from then on assured of all the prizes. That had not been his proudest moment. Had she really not recognised him? Had she too become a writer and was she too experiencing writer's block?

At the table, Fuad and Suzanne let Sabine do much of the talking. Question after question she raised for which she, in the very same breath, provided answers. Her two years in Egypt had evidently filled her with the sentiment that she had strong ties to the country and a deep knowledge of it.

Bored, Fuad decided that his excuse for leaving would be a visit to the dentist. He was waiting for a break in Sabine's torrent of words to get away. When the break came, perhaps divining his intention, Suzanne said, 'I think that we may know each other. If you had a parrot when you were growing up, we do.'

He laughed a touch uneasily and said, 'What a sharp memory you have.'

'It isn't an easy thing to forget. You once brought your parrot to school. You told us that it was a birthday present, that your grandmother had given it to you,' she said.

'Did I really bring it to school?' he mused. 'Frankly, I don't remember.'

'ISIS has taken Ramadi,' announced Sabine, who had been looking at her computer screen during that exchange. 'Will they take Palmyra too? And to think that I had the opportunity to go to Palmyra some years ago but stupidly decided to postpone the trip.'

'I'm sorry but I must leave you now, a dentist's appointment,' he said as he got up. Turning to Suzanne, he added, 'I'll gladly reminisce, tomorrow though. Your memory will refresh mine. So much has happened in the country since our youth that the Egypt of those days seems dead and buried to me, whereas, perhaps not so paradoxically, it may be more alive for those who left.' Then addressing Sabine, he said, 'Good luck with your article. I have no doubt that whatever you're going to write will be fine.'

'Help me with the conclusion,' Sabine said. 'What's your best bet as to what'll happen to Morsi?'

'Martyr or not? Just flip a coin,' he suggested. 'It'll be as good as hedging my best bet.'

'About my leaving Egypt, I would not quite put it your way,' Suzanne said as he was about to go. 'I and others like me were forced to leave; we did not just leave. But yes, the Egypt I knew is still very fresh in my mind. It still is a big part of my dream life. Not a week goes by without my having at least one dream of Egypt.'

'You're right to correct me,' Fuad acknowledged and, before he could stop himself, let out, 'Unlike you, I rarely dream and hardly ever of Egypt.'

No longer in the mood to go roaming around the city, he headed back to his apartment. Why was he so profoundly uninterested in his school mate and recapturing the past with her? Why had he been rude to that young journalist?

Still at some distance from the homeless woman's corner, he caught sight of her squatting against the grocery store's front window.

He took his wallet out of his pocket.

It was only upon coming closer to her that he noticed a tiny parrot perched on her shoulder.

'Hey you, hey you,' the bird screeched on seeing him.

'It's taken you a while,' the old woman observed as she nonchalantly took his twenty-euro bill.

By the time he got to his front door, Fuad had made up his mind to go back home. There was no escaping Egypt and he missed Ali.

On his computer screen was a message from Habiba saying, 'Palmyra will fall into their hands. Palmyra is finished! I'm more convinced than ever that we need Sisi.'

'I can't go back.' He burst out in despair before softly admitting, 'How I love that crazy country!'

When he looked at the computer screen again, there was a fresh message from Habiba announcing, 'Amira just called, she fears that her brothers are coming to town.'

In the afternoon, he lay down to have a nap, hoping to awake calmer.

He dreamt that he was sitting on a wooden café chair, by his side a cup of Turkish coffee resting on a brass coffee table. He was wearing a black suit. Opposite him, sitting in a row on identical wooden chairs and looking very solemn, were Nasser, Sadat, Mubarak, Morsi and Sisi. They too were in black suits and had beside them cups of Turkish coffee set on brass coffee tables. He, as well as they, were there to pay their condolences, but who had died? He did not dare ask. No word was spoken, and other than the coffee sips, no sound could be heard. After every sip taken, he shrank in size and Egypt's leaders grew bigger. He kept getting smaller and smaller and they bigger and bigger. He ought to have been frightened, but he was not. Not only was he shrinking but he was also getting younger, whereas they were getting older. By the end of the dream, he was a toddler and they were as old as Methuselah.

He could hear himself laughing when he woke up – laughing harder than he had in a very long time. It occurred to him that he had Suzanne to thank for that laughter.

Bastille Day

Though she increasingly listened to it with half an ear, Suzanne always turned on the radio first thing in the morning, turning it off only when she went out. It was a presence, a voice she had neither to heed nor to respond to. It was perfect company.

On the radio that morning, much of the talk was about the Greek crisis and America's nuclear agreement with Iran – very little about Bastille Day. Not so long ago, Suzanne would have followed attentively the debates over what Greece ought to do, whether Germany was misbehaving, and who in the match Obama had been playing with the Mullahs had come out the winner. She used to think she had some grasp of what was going on in the world. Now that she recognised she had none, her interest in world events had dwindled, with one exception: events in Egypt, which she was experiencing, surprisingly, as a personal matter. For years, Egypt had been out of her mind before creeping back into it with the onset of old age, which happened to coincide with Egypt's revolution. Ever since, while yearning to pay a visit to the land of her birth and adolescence, she took no steps to make it happen. It was not the country's instability that stopped her. She was not afraid. But to go back after an absence of almost sixty years struck her as inviting disappointment.

Her wavering seemed to have had the effect of heightening her preoccupation with events there. Virtually any news from Egypt – big or small – absorbed her thoughts, so much so that she came to wonder whether her quasi-obsessive focus on Egypt's affairs might be a sign of a failing mind, a precursor of senility.

On Bastille Day, she usually went to the cinema, a habit she was departing from this year, as she was spending the day at home killing time with an Autobridge she had unearthed while rummaging through a trunk. She used to be good at bridge, but had quit playing in her forties.

It was only her second game, yet she was already concluding that there was hardly any bridge left in her. She found it hard to focus on her plays and thought it no excuse that in the back of her mind was Omar Sharif's death and the bombing of the Italian consulate in Cairo. Omar Sharif as an actor had never much impressed her, but as a bridge player he had. She was younger than him – eight years younger. Still, the two of them had grown up during the end of an era, under a dying monarchy; but also at the beginning of a new one, with Nasser's rise to power. She reckoned this put them in roughly the same generation.

Some scenes stay with one forever.

'A lot is in a name,' her paternal aunt had declared over lunch after hearing that Michel Chalhoub had become Omar Sharif. 'Why couldn't he remain Michel Chalhoub?' the aunt had also exclaimed angrily. 'Times have changed, my dear. Success would not come a Michel Chalhoub's way, but it just might for an Omar Sharif,' her father had said, to which his sister had retorted, 'That's precisely my point, he's lending force to the idea that a Michel Chalhoub cannot be considered truly

Egyptian, and that's wrong.' Her father had insisted, 'It's not an idea, it's how things are.' And her aunt had asserted, 'I always thought that Youssef Shahine is not to be trusted, he's had a very bad influence on that boy.' A smug adolescent then, Suzanne used to make a point of remaining silent during those sorts of discussions which, in her eyes, were principally occasions for her family members to state their positions without any intention of budging ever so slightly. That one time, however, she had found it hard to keep quiet and had let it be known that she would much rather be a Nadia or a Mona, or even better, a Zeinab, or a Fatma, than a Suzanne, and that, furthermore, she thought Omar Sharif was an infinitely nicer-sounding name than Michel Chalhoub; besides, he did look like an Omar Sharif. 'But he's not, he's Michel Chalhoub,' her aunt had cried out, smashing a water jug with one too many a vigorous gesture, which had put an end to the discussion. A few months later over another lunch, on referring to his conversion and marriage to Faten Hamama the aunt had sniggered, 'Why are we so surprised? It was to be expected from a man who changed his name from Michel Chalhoub to Omar Sharif.' More for the sake of contradicting his sister than out of conviction, her father had objected, 'But who's surprised? He's a man of his times, free to lead his life as he sees fit.' Not about to give any ground, her aunt had said, 'But what do his parents think of all this? They can't be pleased.' He had countered, 'Success and fame may be all they care about. Success is good, success is beautiful.' Sighing, his sister had lamented, 'I really don't understand why you want to make yourself seem worse than you are.' Laughing, he had replied, 'Little do sisters know how bad their brothers can be.'

A couple of years later, her father had had his Egyptian citizenship revoked and been expelled from the country. A few suitcases, hastily packed, were all the family could take on closing the door of their apartment in Cairo. While they were waiting to board their boat in Alexandria, her burning rage at having had to abandon her collection of books and leave the school where she was a top student had made Suzanne vow never to speak Arabic again and never to return to Egypt, even if begged to come back. 'Perhaps we should've changed our names and converted,' her aunt had blurted out as the boat sailed further away from the coast, causing her father to lose his legendary cool. 'Enough, enough!' he had shouted before murmuring, his voice cracking, 'they wouldn't have let us.'

The Suez Canal War had put a nail in the coffin of an era, allowing Nasser to consolidate his power.

In 1965, Omar Sharif abandoned Egypt for Europe, where he had travelled for film shoots. With its myriad of constraints, including travel restrictions, Nasser's Egypt no longer suited him.

Pushing the Autobridge aside, Suzanne lay down on the floor to do some back exercises, but she quickly gave this up too. It was stifling hot and her fan was not working. Lying very still on the floor, she reviewed in her mind what next to get rid of in her apartment. She much preferred its feel since she had stripped it of all knick-knacks and pictures. It was time for her to turn her attention to her books, as her shelves overflowed with them. Too hot a day for that; tomorrow perhaps, she decided. As for the rugs she had collected over the years, she was not quite ready to part with any. Rugs were her one indulgence. Her desk could go since she now worked at the kitchen table or at the café, the rare times she accepted a translation job. Yes, the desk could go. She would call a charity in the morning to come and pick it up – the sooner, the better. She saw no reason to keep what had become mostly a symbol of a productive life that was well behind her.

She felt herself drifting to sleep. Knowing that she would be awake for much of the night if she let herself have a nap, she got up and began going through her drawers in search of items to be discarded. That mood of wishing to divest herself of her belongings and grow lighter would come upon her often, even as a young woman. When struck by it, she immediately acted upon it and always found something or other to give away, which was why her apartment had gradually become so bare, as had her wardrobe. While examining the contents of her medicine cabinet, she came across a lipstick hiding behind a bottle of disinfectant. She shook her head in disbelief: this was the one and only real lipstick she had ever owned, bought twenty years earlier to impress her last lover. It was a deep red, quite unlike her usual colourless lip gloss. Her lover must have been unimpressed – a few weeks after her exceptional purchase he had made himself scarce. Since then, she had stopped wearing any make-up. She ran the lipstick along her wrist and was surprised to see that it had not totally dried out. 'What was I thinking of, buying it?' she muttered, before throwing it in the paper basket. She was under no illusion. Beautiful she had never been, which turned out to be a blessing in her old age – she had no cause to weep over lost glamour. Without beauty, but not without love affairs. Unaccountably, she had had several sentimental entanglements, none however leading to marriage or permanence. Never having sought either, she was free from regrets.

Other than the lipstick, she found nothing to get rid of in her medicine cabinet, the few medications it contained being well within their expiry dates.

Taking a break from her search for the superfluous amongst her dwindling possessions, she made herself a cup of coffee and sat at the kitchen table. A packet of cigarettes was temptingly close. 'Only ten a day,' she reminded herself and resisted lighting one.

It had been weeks since she had gone to the café. It was silly of her to have stopped going on account of that one encounter with Fuad, her old classmate and rival at school – the boy who thought himself smarter than her even if, more often than not, she got better marks in all the important subjects. 'Now that you're gone, Fuad's definitely top of the class. He'll probably graduate with highest honours. He's not as bad as we thought he was. I'm discovering his nice side,' her best friend had written to her. Traitor! Those words had hurt her at the time. She was struggling in her new school, working inordinately hard to do as well as she had been accustomed to doing at the Lycée in Cairo. And also struggling to get used to Paris – a city she had detested at first, finding it gloomy, sad and heavy. Lifeless compared to Cairo. As for Parisians, she could not get their sense of humour, which often felt mean-spirited to her. To her best friend she had pretended, however, that she loved Paris, writing that it was as glorious and romantic a city as it was deemed to be. That must have rubbed her friend the wrong way who, probably in retaliation, had continued to report to her Fuad's triumphs at school. They had stopped corresponding after a year.

The first time she had seen Fuad walk into the café his face had seemed familiar, but she could not place him. Even after he became a regular there she still could not work out why he seemed so familiar: weeks of seeing him without recognising who he was, and all the while feeling that she knew him. It was the day Morsi was sentenced to death and she had overheard him speaking to the café owner that it dawned upon her who he was.

Voices do not change much. His – deep and full – was distinctive. When she had approached him, he could not have made his lack of interest clearer, seeming to find that neither she nor the young journalist with whom she was discussing Morsi had a right to talk about Egypt. He had given her the impression of expecting anything they might say to be drivel. Giving them the lamest of excuses, he had left them in a hurry. She had barely managed to control her anger at such rudeness. It was not anger flowing from old, unrequited youthful love, her having hopelessly pined for him at school and now wanting some acknowledgement. No, not that at all. The object of her love at the Lycée had been Kamal; Fuad had just been an annoying rival. Still, his shunning her had greatly upset her, causing her to experience a ridiculous but nevertheless intense feeling of rejection. Since then, she was keeping clear of the café, lest he be there.

Some talk on the radio caught her attention. A group connected to ISIS was claiming responsibility for the bombing of the Italian consulate in Cairo. It was all Renzi's fault, the commentator was suggesting – too much tough talk about terrorism. Having walked by the consulate countless times, she remembered it well. A cousin of hers whose mother was Italian used to live nearby. That cousin had been talking about returning to Egypt for ages to research her mother's family history. Were the archives intact? How long would it be before the badly damaged building was open to the public again? The commentator gave no clue, merely stating that the Egyptian government was promising to assume the full costs of the repairs. He then reminded the listeners that the iconic Egyptian actor Omar Sharif had died. This got Suzanne thinking of his change of name. When he was talking to himself, as most people do every now and then, did he say 'Omar this, Omar that', or did he say 'Michel', or did he sometimes say 'Michel' and sometimes 'Omar'? And after he got Alzheimer's, as she gathered he had? Had his parents continued to call him Michel once he became Omar? How would they have felt about him being buried in a Muslim cemetery? In a certain sense, her aunt had been right; his had been far more than a mere change of names. The names Michel Chalhoub and Omar Sharif evoked two different Egypts. By becoming Omar Sharif, Michel Chalhoub was embracing the new Egypt, arguably turning his back on the one into which he had been born. Later, by virtue of leaving it, he would turn his back on the new Egypt too, though he ultimately returned to it and died there, which somehow seemed fitting.

Her intercom ringing interrupted that train of thought.

She picked up the phone.

'It's Fuad.'

'Fuad?' she asked.

'Yes, Fuad, your old classmate.' After a slight pause, he said, 'I'm actually downstairs. Can I come up?' There was silence for a couple of seconds before he went on to explain, 'We were worried about you at the café. The café owner gave me your address. I hope that's all right.'

'Come up,' she said. 'I'm on the sixth floor. There's no elevator.'

'Call the ambulance if I'm not there in half an hour,' he said.

'I warn you, it's hot on the staircase.'

'I'll take it easy, I'll climb very slowly,' he said before adding, '*Tata tata, beshooesh beshooesh!*'

It had been an eternity since she had heard someone say that. If Fuad meant those words to be an olive branch, he succeeded; the words mollified her. It was such a pleasure to hear Arabic spoken by an Egyptian.

It did take him a while to get to her door. She was beginning to worry when she heard a knock at the door.

He went straight to one of her two armchairs and, with a heavy sigh, practically threw himself in it while acknowledging, 'You were right. It wasn't an easy climb. How do you manage?'

'Habit,' she said. 'Besides, it's good for you.'

'Not when it's this hot,' he said.

He did not seem fazed in the slightest by her apartment's Spartan quality.

'You have wonderful rugs,' he said.

She nodded.

'We were quite concerned,' he said. 'You disappeared so suddenly. The café owner said it wasn't like you to be gone for so long. He's very fond of you. He says the café feels strange without you.'

'Well, you can let him know that I'm, well... still alive.'

'Were you travelling?' he asked.

'No,' she answered.

'Were you unwell?'

'No.'

'So why'd you stop coming?'

'Would you like something to drink?' she asked. 'Tea, coffee, a beer, or water?'

'A beer would be great,' he said. 'It's just the sort of day when one craves a beer. Besides, it's Bastille Day, reason to celebrate. But more importantly, we must drink to our unexpected reunion. You must have a beer too.'

She returned with two beers, two glasses and some peanuts.

'That's more than I deserve,' he said.

She handed him a bottle of beer and a glass. 'I'll let you pour it,' she said.

'To us meeting again,' he said as he raised his glass.

She raised her glass.

'I came to make sure you were all right, but also to make amends,' he said.

'Amends?' she repeated after him, trying to keep her voice neutral.

'Yes, amends. I owe you an apology. A big apology! I was rude that day at the café. Nothing to do with you. It was just about me and Egypt, though I will admit that that young journalist got on my nerves. Maybe unfairly so. She seemed so self-assured. It was probably her youth I envied.'

'You seemed to think that we had no right to talk about Egypt.'

He took a big sip of beer and then said wearily, 'The reality is that I don't know where I stand in relation to Egypt, to which I feel bound by a love-hate relationship. Can't live with it, can't live without it.' He took another sip of beer and went on, 'I feel so marginal, I feel excluded, I feel that Egypt has passed me by.'

'You feel excluded? How come?' She was really surprised.

Instead of answering her, he said, 'I'm supposed to know where it is headed, but I don't. I've lost my bearings. I no longer know what to wish for Egypt – what to wish for it that would be realistic at this point.'

'What brought you to Paris?'

He shrugged and said, 'Delusions of grandeur! That's the best way of putting it. My ex-wife said as much, although not quite so bluntly.'

She raised her eyebrows and waited for a fuller explanation. He was not at all what she had expected him to be. She found it hard to relate the elderly man sitting in front of her to the adolescent she had known at school. There was a vague physical similarity and the voice was the same, but the essence of the person seemed to have changed. It could be that she had misjudged the adolescent. They had been too caught up in competing with one another.

'I thought that the government was going to throw me in jail because of some silly article I wrote. Someone told me I had crossed the boundaries within which it is safe to criticise our president. I chose to believe him. My ex-wife tried to persuade me that the government had bigger fish to fry than to go after an insignificant old man like me. I felt I needed a valid reason to leave the country and grabbed this one. It made me feel I mattered, I suppose.'

'So what was the real reason for your wanting to leave?'

'Lassitude, profound lassitude, Egypt had exhausted me.' He paused and reached for his glass before he continued to explain, 'Also, feeling terribly unimportant – impotent, really. I had gotten to the point of having nothing more to say. Thinking about Egypt was like being in a big black hole. I was writing on autopilot. Even that one article I wrote in which I was criticising Sisi. In sum, I wanted to put Egypt behind me. But Egypt sticks, like chewing gum.' Now he laughed.

'Will you go back?' she asked.

'Yes, I will go back. I can't desert my parrot,' he said. 'When we talked at the café, I was amazed that you remembered me bringing it to school.'

'Your parrot is still alive?' she exclaimed.

'Very much so,' he said. 'I count on it outlasting me.'

They both fell silent.

Her desire to hear him talk about Egypt suddenly fading, she got up and said, 'Let me fetch you another beer.'

I must stop talking about Egypt, he thought and closed his eyes. There was no breeze even though all the windows were wide open. None of Bastille Day's brouhaha penetrated the apartment, which faced a quiet side street.

On hearing Suzanne walk into the room, Fuad opened his eyes. Without great conviction, they began reminiscing about their school days but quickly seemed to run out of things to say until he abruptly offered, 'Come with me to Egypt. I'll show you around. I'll introduce you to my ex-wife. She knows Cairo inside out – she's a great guide.'

'I know Cairo,' Suzanne said.

'Of course, of course,' he said, feeling abashed, then he reiterated, 'Come with me to Egypt. I mean it.'

'Thank you. I might take you up on it,' she said, thinking she was very unlikely to.

'We could go for the inauguration of the Suez Canal channel. I could write a laudatory article,' he said, chuckling. 'I hate to confess, but I feel myself become an ardent nationalist when I think of that inauguration.'

'I can understand this' was her response, in a tone he perceived as tepid.

'Time for me to leave,' he said, though there was still some beer left in the bottle.

She did not ask him to stay longer.

After they kissed goodbye, she was unexpectedly sad. From her window, she watched him walk slowly down the street. She thought he looked very old.

Later, she researched Omar Sharif's life on her computer. One article said that, a few years before his death, he had gone to Mecca for the Umra. So he might have really embraced Islam. *Who knows what's inside a person, even the person does not know,* went through her mind as she turned off her computer.

Still later, as she was idly listening to a radio program on the French revolution, the question of what was left of Michel Chalhoub in Omar Sharif struck her as not altogether different from the question of what was left of the Fuad of her youth in the man who had come to see her, or what was left of her own young self in the old woman who wanted to strip her apartment of unnecessary items.

After the sun had set, she went out to buy an ice cream cone. By the time she got back to her building she was toying with the idea of accepting Fuad's invitation.

Right in front of the building's entrance was a kitten so small that she guessed it could not be more than a few hours old. Bending down to pick it up, she could hear faint meowing. 'You're not in luck, I don't care for cats and I can only bear to live with myself. But I think that I have some milk in my fridge,' she told the feather-light kitten as she carried it up the stairs. Once in her kitchen, she gently set it down on the floor. She filled a bowl with milk and placed it next to the trembling creature which drank a tiny bit – far less than she thought it might. Cairo used to be full of rangy stray cats. Had that changed? 'I'll find out if I end up going, but will I ever go?' she mused. A few minutes earlier, she had been genuinely tempted to accept Fuad's invitation, yet here she was, already having second thoughts.

The kitten was lapping some more milk. Should she adopt the poor thing? 'No, no, no! That wouldn't be a good idea, not a good idea at all. Besides, I'm going to Egypt, am I not?' she mumbled to herself. Was indecisiveness a manifestation of deep-seated melancholy, as some writer had said? Had she really read that, or was she imagining she had read it?

'*Beshouesh, beshouesh*,' she told the kitten, now gulping the milk.